The Dedalus Press

<u>Near St. Mullins</u>

John Ennis

John Ennis (signature)

NEAR ST. MULLINS

John Ennis

Dublin 2002

The Dedalus Press
24 The Heath ~ Cypress Downs ~ Dublin 6W
Ireland

© John Ennis and The Dedalus Press, 2002

Cover Design: Simon Webb

ISBN 1 901233 88 X (paper)
ISBN 1 901233 89 8 (bound)

Acknowledgements are due to *Poetry Ireland Review, Céide, Janus* & *Princeton University Library Chronicle* where some of these poems, or versions of them, first appeared. The author is indebted, also, to readings of *Saint Moling Luachra* by Máire B. de Paor, *Kissing the Park*, Mark Peter Hederman, & *Fieldman*.

Dedalus Press books are represented and distributed in the U.S.A. and Canada by **Dufour Editions Ltd.**, P.O. Box 7, Chester Springs, Pennsylvania 19425
in the UK by **Central Books**, 99 Wallis Road, London E9 5LN

The Dedalus Press receives financial assistance from
An Chomhairle Ealaíon, The Arts Council, Ireland.
Printed in Dublin by Johnswood Press Ltd

to Suibhnes everywhere

Some proper names within the text, in alphabetical order:

Alan — an outcast from England whom Suibhne teams up with for a while

Collanach — the priest who saves the newly-born baby, Moling, from death at the hands of his mother. Collanach rears the young Moling.

Eamhnaid — Moling's mother who conceives the saint by her brother-in-law.

Eorann Suibhne's wife

Guaire — Eorann's partner in the wake of Suibhne.

Moling — popular saint, founder of the monastery at present-day St. Mullins, in Carlow, who becomes *anam-chara* to Suibhne.

Mongan — Muirghil's partner who is jealous of her attention to Suibhne

Muirghil — a woman who works in Moling's Monastery, who befriends Suibhne, in the original text, in his last days.

Ronan — cleric whose insistence on land for his Church sparked off the quarrel with Suibhne, who refused him a site on which to build.

Wife of Grac — Grac stole Moling's cow which the Saint needed to further recompense Goban the Builder for his work constructing the monastery at St. Mullins. Grac's wife came begging for sustenance from Moling following the violent death of her husband at the hands of Moling's followers. Moling assigned husband and wife to damnation.

Contents

Metamorphosis	9
Moling's Poems	18
Plight	28
Eorann's Poems	34
The Mill Hag Poems	40
Wandering the Seasons	42
Resolution	60

Metamorphosis

1.

After the debacle
in Ulster
I took to the trees.

Dust of the puffball
I used for wounds,
stems of seakale as a poultice.

Frenzy still splashed
the skies with blood.
I went clean mad.

I'd to find my stormy feet
up in the swaying oaks.
I was my grasping foot.

My forelimbs
lengthened on boughs.
My two eyes widened.

My skull grew diapsid
side windows where my pupils were.
I was arboreal.

Pro-avis,
I did not fly
but glided.

Woods became my home.
One talon from the predatorial
I fed on honey in hollow boles.

I sank back
into my wild avian sockets
many times over.

In the gale-torn limbs
I hung on through each hunt.
Feathers came to insulate me.

Each shrunken minute
felt a million winters.
One day I just flew.

2.

I slid down the tower stairs of evolution
Forced my arms and elbows to adapt to flight.
Where before I'd squat,
My hind limbs now grew adept at perching.

Cute Ronan must have bred in himself a taste for Euclid
The day he drew my new dimension in his mind's eye,
Bird life, cursed to the curve of linear proportion.
But my new cubing gave me godliness.

In my decrease, less heat is squandered.
My chest is pneuma, most of me.
My old boniness is lost in space.

I've earned those broad wings with slatted tips.
I make use of updrafts, winds deflected by hills,
Give praise daily to the physical.

3.

Soaring like the ink-winged gannet, I hang on air.
I've made my own the fulmar's gliding flight
But am as weak on dry ground as a storm petrel,
Rest where the eggs of green plover melt into the scree.
Samaritan to a sandpiper blown in on an atlantic storm.

Say what you will, I'm of a host with Gabriel
Who brought mythic news to a teenage girl.

Ronan's malediction altered my muscle
To keratin, other fibrous protein.

Such metamorphosis in the flesh we're all heirs to
When clouds of depression burn off in the sun.
I'm streamlined for flight and waterproofed.

Any wing is preferable, anyway, to being clipped
Round Moling's door, waiting for the inevitable.

4.

Feathers in contour gloss most of my surface
(The basal portions are downy, insulate).
Major plumes of my wings and their coverts
Function in flight. Imagine my surprise
One dawn at all these feathers growing in tracts!

Feathers burst out of follicles in my skin
Each with its tapered central shaft.

Vaneless feathers whiskered my mouth and eyes.
Bristlelike filters filled my nostrils.

Though I'm well past my prime
, my feathers moulted,
Mocked by pheasant boys in the breeding season,
Juvenile, post-juvenile, first winter, first post-nuptial,

O Moling, why won't you praise each new attempt
       at plumage on me,
Filoplumes, tertials, on the wingbone!

5.

Moling,

You'd sail our rivers and seas with a boat of stone,
But I with my keel, slice blue skies for the taking.
Come, see how my flight muscles attach to it. Saint,

My kneecaps are grown tiny, but not for kneeling.
Radiales of my puny wrists won't raise sword or chalice.
Wishbone weds shoulderjoints to the edge of my keel.

The bones of my forelimbs have settled for flight.
Bones in my hands have long grown into fusion.
Unlike you, I'm at a loss for the functional claw.

Distals allow for the attachment of feathers —
Ronan, see the good you once cursed me with!
Ronan, red cymbal-mouth, you gave me heart.

Marrow deserts me and my wing bones are hollow.
My humerus is coupled now to the air-sac.
My pneumatics are reinforced with bony struts

At points of stress. Wish me luck, then, Moling.
I flex my crackling wrists. My feet have adapted
                                      too much for perching;
When I bend my ankles, my toes bend as well.

Sternum and the good ribs Eorann embraced,
With their old dove-like articulations,
Restructure me as weirdo, wild paraclete.

My weight, as I crouch, clasps me to the branch.
I rise, all feather and femur, shinbone and leathery tendon,
Show you a clean pair of tarsals in the sun.

6.

I spend my spare time at feather care
Spruce up for daily flight.
'Anyone would give you a coin',
Moling says of the tatters on me out in his garden.
Well, when I had family, not to mention Eorann,
On preening, oiling, shaking, stretching, I'd spend hours.

There are, also, the comfort movements.
Lifting both wings upward
Either folded, or spread.
Agitating the whole frame beak to tail.
The monks, who believe in angels,
Think I'm hilarious in feathers.
Wait until they sprout their own
Twitch itchy butts with cherubim.

*

I wish they could hear their bills
Snapping over the scriptures.
But I'm well away from that.

On my flights by the coast
I see the fortune of all flesh —
Gulls, terns, guillemots,
The colonial seabirds
Laying eggs for harvesters
When the moon is down.

My own glory moments are in water.
Winter or summer it's all equal.

With fiery eyes, and straggle of feathers, I mate with the wind.
This, and kicking up the dust on Moling's Quay,
Are the only rituals I feel at home in.

7.

Over the years, I've felt the cardiac
Dimension of what happened to me:
War curse many young endure from first cry or puberty.

Incidentals, date, place of birth, may differ
Not the suffering. The rook-cold jibbing skies
I've made mine, rocked left and right in the wind's

Cradle, seen the same storms wheel those below among the hills
From pillar to post. Murder. Death of my sons, wife, daughters.
I often clove to the filial pines in Eorann's country

High on mountain recesses, my awkward life-questioning
                                              a weight to branches.
And still no answer. Just as there has never been a reply.
Only the voice of the Garbh where the three sisters meet.

So, all that remains is a dual-muscled metaphor —
The pectoralis, which lowers the wing,
Brother muscle, which raises the wing:

These tendon-pulleys keeping us all airborne.
I've long grown cynical of heavenly kingdoms
The coteries of wing clasp and dubious peace.

*

My flesh grows dark from flying for years,
My circulatory system has suffered changes.
Through my left aortic artery has disappeared,

And the right arch channels blood to the dorsal,
My heart's enlarged way beyond human measure
And grows more fearful of the thoughts of men.

For voice, I can manage only these fated gutturals
Where the trachea divides into the bronchial tube,
Vibrations in the membrane with varying tension:

'Eorann, Eorann', my throat the lonesome curlew.
Protest, rage too, at the good earth's dissolution
Where primroses grow as unaware as children

Sacrificed. Syrinx of the territorial.
Kingship has the power of annihilation.
Apocalypse and Armageddon roll into one.

The children of Moira play on the brink.
As I glide by, old bells re-hash the tune.
I carry their traditions, more, in my crop.

I nest less and less, hardly return to Moling,
Live out my days on the homeothermic wing.
Torpor settles on me at night, lifts at sunrise.

More and more, I glide and dip by the coast.
And these are not tears you see. Rather, salt
Excretions from glands above my two eyes.

MOLING'S POEMS

8.

Moling, digger of the millrace for the people, I love you.
Miracle worker.
You raise young girls and boys from the dead.
Day after day,
up to your orphic oxters
in a delirium
of marl at dawn after prayer.
Graip and spade
alternate in your horny fists.

Where are the warring kings today in fire apparel
who hung on your words for peace, reconciliation?
North and south, I could have been one of them.

Callosity is hardening on the spade
along the soles of your feet.
Numbness seizes your perineum and passes.
Mud oozes between your toes.
You squelch in muck up to your thighs.
You drive your circulation through icy veins
till it's time for the Angelus, wintry gruel.

We have our delights. Music at dawn.
I, the water race of wind and light in the sky.
You, the azure of a pool on a fine Sunday.

9.

Dear Moling, the storms that buffet me you know too.
And I have seen your flower-lit sanctuary in its ruin
With all that is mortal of us there consumed in fire
Till we become twin curlew calls in the misty air.

That bright wild boy, you still can see in me
(When I come begging at your lepers' gate for meal)
The child, people say, rested on your bosom once
Illuminating you with his sun-lit countenance.

As I lie here, your weather-beaten face shines down on me.
You recognise in me the One you never were –
Whom Turbulence had entered for a home
And Wildness turned away from every door.

10.

The higher my perch up in the sycamore tree, the stronger will I be
As alter shaman, if scared of heights. O yes, the more ungainly
Crawking visions from a head in which common sense should lie.

True, one can see further from any such high and hilarious perch.
But you, onlookers, just can't wait; you hang on for my next lurch
Down. The drum of my own thought I cut from the living larch.

Still, I depend on your brittle fingers twigging every bough
For a few precious seconds longer. You know how life is anyhow.
One day I imagined Eorann hung out dry white clothes for me
                                                           on low

Branches at home, but I merely flew over a holy bush near
                                                Moling's well.
Some days less wholesome tatters the lay monks raise up
                                                  for the gale,
Like the afterbirths of calves, for a laugh, lusty fellows that they are
                                            in the soul.

From the sycamore I saw Moling, naked in his room without his
                                                christian oils
Or his fanciful trappings, his alb, his cincture, his golden chasubles.
I flew away when his lonely fingers worked at his boils.

Love, like a noble oak, goes up in forest flames. I see my skull
Fallen on the cut-away as bleached as the remains of any seagull.

11.

Let it all hang out
Let it all hang out
               Moling
Let it all hang out
Let it all hang out

God on your knee
A seven-year old fondled, all night
        Moling
And was that paradise?
The angel raging.

His sword in flame
you in a flap
        Moling
Back to the monastery
Barked the wings

And it is a terrible thing
To see a man
        Moling
Cursing a woman
A child on her back

I saw the woman
Hang from a tree
        Moling
Worm in her eye.
I pecked her flesh. I was hungry.

To leave a child, motherless
To leave a mother, childless
        Moling
Is as bad as a shattered abort
Kicking in a bin.

You hold up the daily bread
There is blood on it
          Moling
You don't see it, but I do.
A terror, to eat this bread and flesh,
Moling

12.

Moling,

Feeder of the hounds
A loaf of bread with butter
      for each mouth.

Their masters on horseback
Look worried at your words.

Would you subvert our nature?

Feeder, too, of the dog foxes
Vixens and their cute cubs,
Intercede for us

that our snarls
disappear
in the whorl
of a flower.

13.

The old red poppies
at the meadow's edge
watch them drowse
and rave

in the half-light
of their days.

Foreboding shakes
the goldfinch
on the tall thistle
whom no breeze
agitates.

Moling,
keep the meadowers
at their prayers.

14.

Live man,
taste clay.

Well, no great miracle there, Moling
for, consider your sick swine
(so close to us, it's said,
our two hearts are interchangeable).

They nose up the grass sod to lick the paddock soil,
the darker traces of our twin elements.

Pray hard, then, friend,
                      Moling

savour all the words
we said
or did not say
or ever will
or must.
Helpless as birdshrieks
in the gathering dusk.

15.

Moling's graviportal at their psalters
ponder the oddity I am in flight
not knowing their own altars

demise in time,
recorded by Gabriel.
Large, flightless ones, heavy-boned divers,

they opt for the rational.
Pneumatic in my bird bones
I grow easy in the soul.

I am.
That is
all there is.

Do not seek of me
a lasting fossil.

16.

Moling,

When I collapsed within your walls, in tears I said,
'This is home.'
I was tired with the tensed tiredness of days
Early mornings flying to murder. Late nights
Desolation the last thing I heard in branches.
Mid-day hassle and pain in an addled brain
Tidier than any saint's.
A lone crow was cawing up in your pine tree.
A cowering of alder withered beneath your oak.
The brown leaves of your beeches chattered like pilgrims.
I came to the beautiful sandstone of your chapel door
Where I'm told I'll breathe my last in this story.
I got wind of your sanctuary and the wide Barrow.

You said,
'Be thankful, calm, come rest out in the sun.
Child, see as far as the tarmacadam age.'

Sandy soil settled on the fresh grave of a boy
To the left inside your cemetery wall.
'Give us time,' you said. 'We will be spared.
Fold your wings. Take these gentle scenes to heart:
Cooing of woodquest up in my ash tree.
Rasp of spades in newly-tilled soil.
Spring cabbages heeled in before the frost.
A dog barking at my milch cows on the hill.
Give us time. But you will be speared!'

Then I saw all the dead crowding round your door
And I cried, 'This is not my house', the graves like sardines.
The dead jamming your doorway with their stone crosses.
I see the old weathered ones toss to and fro.

As the earth moves in an aeon, you can see them move.
Your people should be long embraced in clay, who expect to be
          that step ahead
At the resurrection. Get the leg in first. The first
To be recycled amid the dust of galaxies
Decades after our lives and the red dwarf in the sky.

Moling,
I flew in here seeking the easy fix.
There is no resolution except to oneself.
Even on this warm, sunny, September day the Garbh
Funnels up the valley between Brandon
     and the white-bouldered hills.

Let this place be my compass point, then, that pierces
For I cannot live without the caress of clouds
Circling the small of the back of Brandon

Or my drift and glide down the tender belly
Of the wind, or across Tramore, dunes smooth as shoulder blades.

I'll write a poem on your life, forward it thirteen hundred years
From 696 when you first chose the sandstone.

I cannot abide this sanctified ground of bones.
Each day my business is to fly away from you,
Moling, as far as turn back.
To Aran, Bun Abha, overnight on Ben Bulben
Settled in the ivied fork of a tree for warmth,
Watch you within preen yourself up in prose
Above the water glistening on the Barrow
The smell of water, and the air off water.

PLIGHT

17.

I have seen your gashed faces advancing towards me
From the reddened no-man's-land where I left you to die:
All those that I laid low, once, with my various swords.
Or, if I did not have a sword, well, with my iron words.

You lance at me in leafy nightmare up the barely-lit boughs
Of beech and oak, of ash and sycamore. Your blood-shot eyes
Shake me at all hours even in the gentle placid summer
Nights of the hive in an old tree trunk where bees murmur

Distil honey below me in the short, dark hours.
       So many gaping wounds,
The hurts I inflicted! I cannot push away your raucous
       dying sounds.
Crowds at Moira look up in hate at me as they stream
       out of Samhain masses.

Widows, orphans, the like, flail at my low spent wings
       in mountain passes.

All I know, day in day out, is the mild pouring rain.
I have leant on reeds, too, and I have felt their pain.

18.

Once a king
now I peck the fields for grubs
like my ancestors did.
I am become so small in my own estimation
any labourer could slice my skull off with a sickle.
I wouldn't mind but it would be no good
to demand such ease so early.

Judgements stand like beech
in Winter
excoriated
gale after gale.

I cry into the humble earth
how long
how long.

19.

A cleft round home in the flank of the Gravelly Hills.
A wide burrow where two badgers were battered to death.
Hollow in the groin of an elm I hid in for a whole year.
Then, in a mountain grotto where summer lingered
                                      like a girl rock-climber.
A dried font with beech leaves in a deserted chapel.
Anything half-inviting, retort,
  adequate in diameter, tubular, humming, out of the gale.

Shelter

Thought I might meet
warmth, one night of permanency. A dry bed.
Always a dupe to casements, pavements, doors.
Nests lined with the little pebbles I could heat
what dirt, dried moss I could muster in a rush.
Sticks, leaves, lichens, clabber, rootlets, algae.
I beaked in ewe fibres, strands of couch grass
       all around me.
I was a sight but worked past heartbreak with none to see me.

I made fast the felt with mud. Lip drivel.
On a windy ledge, like semi-detached. Each nest
for a time a lasting city.

20.

I have wept with those who cannot find affection,
The millions who exist without the tender word,
Who trawl from dawn to dark the seventh ocean
Below me or are beaten back into the callous herd

At every gap. Few find it, this pearl of shocking price;
Long before and after Love a great tenderness lingers.
We are but poor prostitutes left alone with our cries
Who caress, stroke heaven with their fragile fingers.

We have shouldered the tyrannical put down and the jibe
At the hive entrance, the last degradation of the drone.
We know the heart, the thought patterns of the tribe,
The intimate knowledge of limbs not all have known.

I cried once with the rest, but with them come to the end of tears.
I pass each night in futile words, and in futile words my years.

21.

Even

   the swallow feeds with widening gape
   when June to August is insect laden.
   The warbler gleans food from the fools' parsley
   by any roadside,
   the eagle flexes talons and beak for the lamb's dissection.
   The heron, the spear and trigger in the gracious neck
   along the fish pools of the Barrow,
   the kingfisher plunges into the Nore for silvered morsels,
   the bill of the Suir wader probes mudflats for worms.

But
   for that cursed invertebrate, man on the wing,
   cast out from his family, mostly famine forage.

Leaves and buds in the craw in the greenleaf season.

The rave of nectar

haws ripe in nutrition

just to keep him on air.

22.

There were others on the same branch as ourselves
well, not so much that same branch most times
but at discreet distances around, above and below
adjoining oak, red rowan, the latest forests with fancy names.
Road resters, the grove whingers, the alder stragglers.
Wild roosters with no dawn to crow into.
How one yearned for a wing touch!

And, even, if in the dark, or the self's half-light
one reached out across the toppling branches
and there came a brushing together of feathers, or an embrace
with beaks, it was all over with the transience of daybreak
with a wing out of joint for good measure.
Or a tender vulva refusing to relocate.

Or, maybe, two would take off into the skies
to the chattering and good wishes of some wedding chorus
in a calm mind with fair weather, as if these
were the norm and a little excitement tippling the leaves.

Of course, one longed for the real thing, the great migrations.
Sailing on the updraft of one's companions and peers.
Wing tip to wing tip, the unspoken communion.
Or those honking geese in a V before the snow comes.
Whirring of swan wings across turlough and pasture.

But we didn't dare aspire to such grandeurs.
Give us always our distance, the necessary distance
as we plot our destinies from fledgling nest
      to the last clawstop.
Detached, at best, with the least putting in on anyone.

Eorann's Poems

23.

I have seen the tacking of your white linen out on clothes lines.
I have seen it in full sail in the brisk, dry winds
        from the four horizons.
I have seen you take the sheets in with armfuls white
          as sunlit drifts of snow.
I have seen, sweet Eorann,
    how life goes on.

Our children dart among the apple trees after Bran.

There carries up to me yelping of kennels on a frosty dawn.

I see my stripling boys feed the leaping wolfhounds.

And I am so far removed from their abusive eyes,
I grow as small in their teenage estimation
As that gull gliding to the north over Moira.

I would go over Eorann's and then not go.
Some days can but poorly navigate on air.
Wherever I am I remember the triple orchards
      hung with blossoms, or fruit.
The full pewter vessels on the oaken table.
My tunics folded in the deep press by the fire.
The one with the broken clasp is absent since the battle.
On the morning of Moira it came off me in your hands,
Soon featured as a scarecrow to please the children.
Raidéog now scents Guaire's linen with your own.

Before, during, and after each war and skirmish
Many voices could have brought me home.
I am powerless to risk that all over again.
I am no more believed with flowers.

There might have been a convergence of thought,
      of winds on a bitter morning.
If I swoop low now your face
Wounds me to the marrow.
Our cultured honeysuckle is forsaken and grows wild.

And, then, the breeze out of nowhere pulses.
I rest becalmed in your eye,
Or so I seem, for a minute.
Fly off all over the place.

24.

Eorann, you left out for me a vesselful of water.
I thought it worthless at first sight
Until the news of my thirst hit me.

You spoke to me in my summer drought.
In the beginning I thought your pewter
Was a mirage brimming nothing more.

You'd seen me forlorn in the dry paddock,
Floundering to reach a dry spring.
My thoughts were cracked, my senses, swollen.

What men will do in drought,
What words they'll say!
I could not even whisper, 'Water, Water'.

Today when you spoke
Your words moved like palm trees.
The water's like your graceful hands about me years ago.

25.

I have seen the goddesses of the Hesperides
(The girls Moling told me were dead and buried).
I saw their bodies blossom
      in the moonless night.

After that who would embrace a May dawning
When to nest in triple boughs was edenic rapture?
I felt their golden apples in the dark.
How beautiful they were, how beautiful!

The horned snake coiling up around their tree
Was as inevitable as you and I,
Eorann, once, in coitus, in the sunset

Islands of other evenings, old Hesperides.
The juices welled in us, the times we had.

This tree whom Moling's willing axeman sunders
Greens still from its graft base in abundance.

26.

Apple trees in bud.
Exquisite
was the thrust
of my shaft
into your
paradise.

Walking up
the garden avenue
in the month of May
once at home.

The pippins
in blossom.

Our heads in the
air for the scent.

27.

The months stretch out like dying since Eorann.
This summer's January days blow wet and long.
I know now the mateless dimension of any person.
Cave after cave I've entered without praise or song.

Years pass. I wait for your twin soul. A flight that sings.
I could not hold you anymore than I could the swallow.
For, at the thought of frostiness, you took to your wings.
You plot your own instinctual skies, your own tomorrow.

I seek you in oak clearings. On southern shores. By inland lakes.
I have begun to despair. Will I ever see your face
Again, or those slender movements your body makes?
Craving you is my punishment in blue empty space.

One day, I'll maybe sense sunshine. Excitement in the air.
      Concepts like dry summer. Freedom. Choice.
Who knows? Soon after that I'll hear your voice?

28.

The folly of loving you, Eorann! How all is void:
Our human battlegrounds where there is nothing
Of love to be relied upon. No truce congenial as bread.
Only all the lonely faces that die alone, fearful, frothing.

I'd say there are few poems in your nature
And these, my distant aberrations, leave you cold
Or hardly touched at all. And my future
With the crowd at Moira is very much on hold.

And, then, I see celebrations weep October hedges
Our affairs on ancient thorn, the ornate briar,
Profligacy of leaf written over the edges
Of turbulent streams and I grow muted. Dear,

Too many seasons lie in us waiting to be read.
Tenderness of position, when we had a bed.

29.

How shall I face, then, this inner immolation
The flames that lick the heart, the fuel
Igniting as it spreads across creation.
You seep into my soul, explode with a force that's cruel.

All year I've seen our companionable galaxies burn out
                 in desolate skies.
Eorann, after my last departure, the few words of friendship,
I yoked to each falling morsel and meteorite my cries
Strangled them in my throat before they'd reach my lip.

So, love, I touch off, add to my life the June-dried fossils
Of frozen forests and stars, each private desolation.
Infinities of far collapsing suns will soon suck in all the ills
We shall ever come down with now, and each old fond elation.

Eorann, in memory, lean across with honey on your finger
To salve this charred spirit, please do so, please linger.

The Mill Hag Poems

30.

A quilt of stinging ants was more welcoming than her voice.

The yelping of hounds after the dog fox,
more benign.

A hailshower at the close of day, a night-time sheet of whiteness.

Torrents from a hillside in a wintry glen,
a warm scented bath.

The rusty nail of her voice and the mallet
of her will were well matched.

The sourness of her words curdled the wholesome milk
      in the udders of dawn.

Yes, better the whinge and the whine of the wind
      than any endearment of the hag in mid-winter.

31.

She sinks into a wizened piece
and everyday her claw-edged teeth
bite deeper into me.
Her every greeting is a scythe.

The north-east winter wind is kinder
than her breath.
The rasp of her tongue
lingers like a thousand frosts.

And when she weeps
her acid tears
raise boggy mists
in every sound I make.

The soggy land becomes my voice
my sanctuary the woolly sallies
more curlew
then the curlew waters.

Leap borrows leap.
Word borrows word.
I leave her at my back
like a wing-broken bird.

Wandering the Seasons

32.

Eanair

Like me, Mary,
Not taking the main road for fear of stoning
You are smelt out by zealots and the jackals of Juda:
Here,
Enough blue in the sky for the cloak of a young mother
Who walks the windswept bandit hills to Elizabeth.
Saviour to be, her foetal darling
Knees to his chin soon in the warm amnion
Ready to kick at intimate greetings, embraces.
Both of you free from Joseph, his screaming wife
Like a lioness and their gawky children.
You walk alone, your only companions
The buzzards swooping in Judean passes.

Moling, your mother, too, who bore you, illegitimate,
Eamhnaid travelled by night for fear of detection,
Delivered you in a snowstorm with drifts a man's height
Her forearm round you in the snow to smother you,
Her hand reaching for stones in the snow to brain you,
Hang in there, no woman, no cry. Darkness all round
Creator, the One. His dove came to melt you a clearing.
Collanach came on you, whom gossips dubbed your father,
Took care of your rearing like the surrogate carpenter.
So, you were not one more doomed embryo on statistical waters
On boats cleaving the night waves, or in wing-bent skies,
Those on whom a clinical tide recedes in dismemberment.

Here, on this mild day for the time of year
Linnets flock over Moling's dykes, larks trouble
Last Autumn's stubblelands.
Gnats dance round thorn bushes on a mild forenoon.
Furze, groundsel and deadnettle bloom.
Rosemary in a mountain coign.

Peace

The doe rabbit resumes her nursery where the clay rises.
Three whole nights since last the dog fox passed.

Peace
Plover crowd the marshes
A woodquest from a pine tree
Talks of inner calm to me.
Pollen dusts the yew.
      Hazels droop their male catkins.
      The woodland floors erect with hyacinths.

But storms, gales any day soon for the gulls flock inland.
The snow will chide with white the gleaming chestnut bud
(Yesterday the blue skies came drifting with white flakes).
Rain will whiten its sunlit judgement on flooded pasture,
      pool and torrent.
At every cross, mud and morass from passing wheels.

Mary,
Hear our voices as we fly daily toward our destinies.
Most beautiful mother, protect us on the path, on the road
In the womb and in the skies.

33.

Feabhra

Male redwings sing their way to silence.
Pilewort explodes into stars.
The larch is tipped with amethyst.
Hazel and yew are gold with dust.
Coming into Candlemas,
The coltsfoot sets its flower stalk like a flag.
I've time to contemplate these and the first primrose
      by Moling's well
Before the water carriers abort me into flight.

You would have grown to manhood many times over
Long ceased to be old Ronan's young psalmist.
Everywhere I see your face and the hurt I caused you
When my spear pierced you deep below the breastbone.
I killed God and man the day I killed you.

That being so, life goes on
The clay has long filled your beautiful eyes
There is not a night but I think of it and the embraces
That would have been yours, children to follow.
Storms cleanse the budwings from the tree.
The earth alters colour in us at a violent rate.
White frost, then snow, then an aggressive green.
An army of dogberry advances in red on me.
The act I freely did drives me mad over Moira.

Floods disappear from the sun-mirrored Curragh.
Galls on the great oaks of Doire turn to russet.
A turned lea goes ash-grey in dry wind.

I must be robust for hard times ahead.
Herons leave their island nesting places
Feast at dawn on Moling's mill-race frogs.

I never knew your name.
I weep for you, but the earth is in your mouth.
You cannot utter the words to release me.

And, so, I wonder if ever, if ever.
Then, by my side, a little yellowhammer sings.
Sandmartins come back to rent my cliffs.
Willows grow white with bud and catkin.
The tortoise shell leaves its mummy state.
The birch spreads over me its lacy foliage.
The aspen is all about me in pale amber.

Young man, my lines will never bring you round to life again
Even if new grasses whisper and bend in the wind.

34.

Márta

Peace on this first morning
As if the snow and the east wind had never been
Or the harsh words spoken, Eorann.

The pines recoil, then again plunge.
Young sycamores lift their battered pre-leaves from the soil.

Blackthorn buds toss this white-tipped way and that with flower.

Each noon now is shortening its oaken shadow.
We were our own triangle, you, me and the children.
Herons feed the little elvers to their young.

The chevril is in white blossom
By our thousand pathways,
Eorann.

Cowslips multiply. Your wild garlic grows tall with green leaves.
Wild arum snares the young March flies.

Young lambs are born at night in your fields, Eorann.
Or as dark approaches, and in the first dawn
For day marauds with enemies.

The anniversary of His conception and our son's is any day now.
The swans grow yellow from the silted tide.
The cricket opens its summer doors again. Eorann,
The ivy berries prepare a feast for me
Within earshot of the fowler.

A blackcap whistles in our sally covert.
The crowfoot plays out its gold.
Yes, Eorann, there was another
I could have kissed, known forever, if I did not lower my eyes.
Now a curlew repeats the liquid calls of all loves lost.

Jackdaws move in squads collecting sprigs,
Build their high nests in the tall ash trees.
Even the rush flowers with sex, Eorann.
The first female wasp tastes the sunshine, Eorann.
Hedge sparrows build in thickets near our doors.

The blackthorn is your white trousseau! Our twin cherries
                                                        bloom!
Here, a wild bright day on the south-eastern coast.
The cold winds come whipping the blue sea to white.

March moves out to its own accompaniment.

35.

Aibreán

Alan, this brisk day is an interlude.
The earth is nursing a first orchid.
Remember how we met that morning
The tortoise shells shook off their torpor
And the sloe coverts were powdered white.
A year on and we have made our own the hazardous skies.
I became your eyes and your eyes were mine.
White butterflies drift through the sloe blossom.
Neither yet knows bitterness.

Ours dissipates and, even if death comes,
There is the kinder truth in what we see and hear:
Goslings in a yard; the sallows in white.
Snipe call. Swallows visiting old nests. Cuckoo call.
Seagulls leaving well-fed tillage for their nesting grounds.
An otter lazes on a sunlit reed-patch by the river
Where old brown reeds fall in marshy places.
The drone of insects accompanies the Angelus.

Along miles of pathway, the wild violet purples.
Mason bees are out! The first of the little copper butterflies!

In the copse where we rest, fold our wings
Nettle and wild holly provide Brendan
Cordage for his sails, waterproof his stern.
Out in the open, rough soil gapes with thirst.
The blue skies hoard their rising showers.
We knew this glary morning would not hold.

Faraway an axe fells an elm for boat and plough.

Our eyes wait as if for corn shoots to germinate.
Wars of wind and frost pass over them daily.
Slan lús, old styptic, darkens the hill grasses.
The wounded cried out for it after Moytura.
They are all at peace now. Ours is to come.

Soon we will be winging up toward the futile heavens,
Bank to separate sky-roads, this place a memory.
Each fibre in our sally thicket is softer than white thistledown.

36.

Bealtaine

Guaire, guard her and my care well in this time of nurture.
Wood pigeons teach their young to fly
Luring them through intricate forest branches.

Leverets feed independent of their mother.
The night sky is the daisied floor of paradise.

The blossoms of any apple trees are industrious,
Saxifrages tutor my rocky scree. Guaire,
White draws its coverlet over the rowan I sleep in.
Squirrels drill into the old brown oaks.
Gardens of fraughan romp in the yellow moorlands.

The swelling river bears the breeding swan.
Swallows refurbish, warm old nests again, re-mate.
If hawk or kestrel take them in flight, bereave their young
Neighbouring birds take on their brood indoors. Guaire,
Broom outshines the rocky furze on chaliced headlands.

Every inch of soil, too, is a school of life.
Why do I hurt then, Guaire? Eye for an eye?
When I returned to her the last time I was not even noticed.
It was as if I had never existed.
Here is no earthly perfection. Nor can there be.

Yet, though my mid-May skies be laden
Chestnuts light their candelabra night and day.
Clovers come in deep-rooted purple.
The hazel is a satchel honeycomb.
Young badgers play round their setts like lambs.

Guaire, the cuckoo's call is faint with mist and rain.
Alder is blessed for me in communion white.
Guard me the tender green of my fledgling beech
For leaves are whipped and whirled in sleety winds.
Pond weed fills the old marl hole and bird-lime pit.

Bittersweet, travellers' tree and lilac must burst out.
So it is with family and the sloe nurses its swelling fruit.
Guaire, weed out the poisonous dropwort where it roots,
Cultivate arbutus and juniper on my southern hillslope
Where wrens link up woodland margins with their song.

37.

Meitheamh

Perfection has come today across these earthly hills
As the last nippy hail shower billows the growing swathe.
I fly above a surfeit of rainbow and of song.

Come from the woods out into this bright foliage with me.
Your shadow will soon be nil at noon
Standing amid the brief gold aureoles of the plantain.

Partridge broods fly alongside me full of childish wings.
A kingfisher parades beneath the alders, the warm river silences.
I rest an hour beside the snowcrop's shining stars.

Butterflies, daymoths below me are specks of snow and flame.
Swallows skim the racing meadows in advance of rain.
Wild camomile speaks to me of apples and their ripening.

Flying, I love the mild rain showers, drenched crowns of trees,
Cry of wild duck, a hedgewarbler singing in wet bracken,
The snipe's goat call that fills the twilight mist.

The cranebill's crimson now, the buttercup's yellow gold.
The mountain ash on every slope fades to motley berry.
The blackberry weaves its thorn about the innocent bloom.

The waterlily's a voluptuous white in the boggy stream.
Sapphire beetles multiply. Young thistles litter pastures.
Speedwell blooms bright blue among the meadow grasses.

My wild strawberries redden a little more each day.
I see Eorann gather speedwell for the venison.
I feed on tender watercress around the madman's well.

Blue lightning rips round me near St. John's Day.
I cower with fraughauns on the ripening heath
Till the June moths rise again all jet and crimson.

I wish my children joy in the brief blood of the stars
As pod and pouch, sack and purse, swell in a hundred species,
Prepare for the leap and spring to scatter, scatter everywhere.

The Moira hills are whitening with clover.
Waterhens chatter on as usual. Poppies bloom.
Stoats decimate young broods. That kind of world too.

Below me a man pulls hemlock to cure his leprous ear.
Child of grace, I cannot reach to you with a bulb of iris
      for your toothache.
Scarecrows eye the day's dead on a summer esker.

38.

Iúil

The horsefly ekes out a full chalice from the vein.
The wolf-foot is in bloom, where rabid wolves decline.

The dogviolets are white, the hazelnuts are white.
Owls and poor lepers lament all the sultry night.

The foxglove is a purple spike in a Moira sceptre.
Flying across meadows of plenitude, I'm an aborted spectre.

Ragwort in abundance marks the earth's gold hoard.
Tremendous heat stills the voice of thrush and blackbird.

The cornfields change from olive green to yellow.
The bitterness in the crab-apple begins to mellow.

I sleep in the pink fields of Odin by the sea
Or, companion to the goldcrest, up in his inaudible ash tree.

Bees still swarm and hum
Across the sunset roses of wild hypericum.

39.

Lúnasa

I saw him walk through yellowwort on the hills of Thomond.
Glorious he was, immortal, as he loitered round.

He was everyman, alone, everywoman and no one
Till a red rowan grew up through his mangled forehead
       in that vision.

I heard, too, how he howled when they took him for circumcision
And quietened only in the grandfatherly arms of Simeon.

But now this hair was John's wort in its oiled and tasselled gold.
The Magdalen was with him like tall Angelica, let it be told.

At their feet a chaffinch tweaked the fallen wheat to chaff.
They gathered betony, crowberry, heard furze pods explode.
       I heard them laugh.

Raspberries still held themselves red for them, the wild bees,
       their liquid store.
The centaury, its pink. Honeydew was running on the sycamore.

Leaf by tender leaf, birches turned to gold in his hands
Above the sheepfolds on the saffron lowlands.

The world like a fretful spinning midge rolled on in space.
But they left me a little peace of mind in that empty place.

40.

Mean Fómhair

The sally disrobes in golden winds
And fallen angels if there be some, come drifting down
		in ones and twos from the larch.
The dogwood grows carmine.
Woodbine blooms in a reddening hawthorn.
Hazel woods wake up to their catkin sex.
The ivy blossoms for Moling's honeybees.
White frost nips the tips of apple branchlets.
Crimson is kindling on the pyrebound rowan.
Birch leaves throw a coverlet over my child's cradle.

Whispering winds gather over the greying stubble.
A great moon swells in the pewter sky at twilight.
Beneath it our games are decided. Winner takes all.
I see a small ball reach skyward, hear a distant cheer.
Yes, it's that time of year. Rival colours adorn the raths.
Grass clusters by the furze clump hide the hunted hare.
Rooks roll, bank and tumble by me in the hot sunny air
Feed on the glittering red berries of the wild water alders.
Like Seraphim, the wild geese move across my errant skies.

Gulls, the summer of sun and storms of rearing over
Move inland beneath me to the empty cornfields.
A pair of eager partridge quarrels on a slope.
Finches pierce the knapweed for its oiliness.
A goldcrest flits through my buckthorn thicket.
Woodcocks breast the brisk mid-month weather.
Peacock butterflies light on the Candlemas daisies.
Robins and wrens test out their autumnal notes.
Eagles visit the ledges I rest on up the mountain.

Calm days. Mists. Two days since I saw a tortoise shell!
Why are the oaks still green down in the river valley?
A deeper bronze overtakes each beech and sycamore.
Herds graze and sleep and graze. Quiet alternations.
Everywhere a marriage of bird life and abundance.
Food on branch and twig. A hearth of sunlit days.
Absence of storms. Flocks that come with storms.
Grey crows gather alongside me on the upper slopes
As September nears its end with blue-sky weather.

41.

Deireadh Fómhair

Now is the time of completeness for me.
I shall not know such community again
Until I've crossed into the eternal hills.
Your wars today over in Moira! So long ago!
The redwing, bird of frost and snow, is come.
I eat the glittering berries of solanum,
Drink where otters sport in turbulent waters.
My eucharist is shared edible fungi on a forest floor.
I see his blood in the rare orchids.
His ousel leaves the streamlet's side.

Nature sits down now to its last supper.
Hares feed on fallen apples and, with people,
Share tasty roots rising from the ground.
The hedgehog furnishes his winter kitchen.

Red squirrels run copse to copse for food.
For them October polishes each hazelnut.
Horse chestnuts lie in their fallen cradles.
The spear of the wild iris is broken in me.
My words are no more than the badger's runic claws
On Moling's oak by the tall white skeletons of archangel.

Will I see ever again the first primrose?
Meet her round the entrance to the rockface?
Nightly, sex-scenes of mating foxes, where the furze divides.
Wild barnacle geese cry out overhead.
Dead shrews litter Gethsemane paths.
The stoat is swift on track of rat and mouse
And snipe zig-zag across the fallen leaves.
No butterflies anymore.

But hollyberries are reddening by the hour
As rooks visit old nests, all poise and ebony
      in sunlight above the trees.

So, let innumerable webs drape bush and hedge,
The old flowers rust with age, do not cry
If the short day nurses its blooms in vain.
Above our heads the lowly heavens wave
With constellations definitive as grain.
Our chaff will scatter like the summer pollen,
Our children pick wild yarrow for the passover.
Somewhere Eorann roasts the hazelnuts
Crunches into the apple of immortality,
As a donkey brays nearby in a sodden acre
Whose forebear bore my love into Jerusalem.

42.

Samhain

They say the blackberries are poisonous
So I had better not, Muirghil.
November's rainbows arch over bleaker winds.
Sunset lingers before the darkest night.
I forage for food, fragile warmth
As a wand of vermilion fades above the valley
Where old trees stood crippled in crimson flame.
Even the Barrow and its pools were of Cana wine.
The pigeons were birds of paradise in flight.
A penultimate peregrine roamed in burnished plumage.
Then charcoal trunks of shadow filled the fields.

I was tempted to stay forever in the rowan hills
With blackback gulls shrieking in the blue, windy sky.
But sleet soon turned to white, prolonged snow showers.
The north wind whistled away the last brown leaves.
The hunters' moon added new glimmer to the frost
And I knew cold and freezing like never before.
The cry of the Garbh shook even the oaks to the root.
Grey crows watched for victims drifting on winter floods.
Which is why I pecked round your door, Muirghil.
My airs and graces were gone, my humiliation was complete
To drink my morning gruel from a cowpat.

This, within sight of Moling and religion.
My gut stiffened. I was yet able to hate you
And all that sin-song place stood for in me.
Somehow I lifted myself up into the sky again
To rest with grouse defiant on a heathered slope.
Watched philbin sweep into the valley, among whom

Audacity, with spiked helmet, is king
Flew mile on mile of luxuriant green fern;
On St. Martin's Day saw shoals of herring.
More pleasant to me the natural choirs, the finches
In the oaks, redwings on the ivy-creepered trees
And the bass-voiced crow's unfettered harmonies.

I still had a garland or two of herbs
To grace the watercress, first ivy berries,
Spleenwort with its sickles, saxifrage with kidney leaves.
The missel thrush was celebrant in the white sunshine.
The swart sloe glistened through its yellowing leaves.
If the blackbird still had a modicum of music
In his golden beak, I retained an elemental pride in mine.
We fed on fuschia berries the frost had flavoured.
Wimbrel passed by us on the way to an old stubble.
I prayed to be chervil, which knows no winter,
Yet looked like heron, sculpted, motionless.

43.

Nollaig

The winds have cleansed the boughs of winter foliage
So there's more light and moisture for the April bud.
Ronan's in the news. My parole is denied until my death
For the evil that I did. What drives us to do mad things?
Why does misfortune dog one family, not another?

This morning, the pitiless cold wind was harsh, Moling,
As biting, final as your words to Grac's wife and child.
I saw them stagger from your presence, bowed and cowed.
Alone, they set their few beans and futile winter wheat:
A pietà to be, where plover call out plaintively.
Now emptiness is all where the swallow soared.
The blossoms of the furze are filmed with ice.

Mongan with his spear lies in wait for me.
His eye rules the world with retribution, he
Matches brown leaves and snowflakes in the swirling wind.
I had better take care. Life is always perilous.
The river embraces the sky in its grey mood.
Black slugs devour the fallen crab apples.
I can't fly on. I must fly on, take courage
From the December moth that begins its little life,
Solace in the citrus smell of the noon-thawed gorse.
On the plain new wheat slants in the brief blue wind.
A single dandelion blossoms, whom no bee visits.
A gathering of linnets marks the passing of the year.

On this your birth night
Redbreast and sparrow feed with me in the moonlight.
But I would to God I was under Moling's roof, at his side
To drink his milk with arum root, his food for invalides.
Yet I am as isolated as the cormorant
Sleeping inland on tree-covered islands.
I remember a time in our home, Eorann
The day with milk and saffron we chased away the measles
      from our children.
When I see the little greve, floating in their pondweed
Nests on reed-fringed pools, I think of my children.
We were Godhead and daylight to those children.
Our homes, like the hedgewarblers', hang on reeds.

Resolution

44.

I grow old, grow old, superfluous
my belly gone oedematous
incubate the last few poems
cocooned like eggs below the viscera.
These struggle out, soft touch, naïve,
brooded over and over. I regulate
the heat they'll need to wing
across the fowling generations.
Sons will sink down into their fathers' arms
praising them.

See how it hatches out, your poem!
    Downy. Beautiful.
In your palm a wonder,
    and eternal.

45.

Keep with me a minimum distance to breathe
like that flock of swallows spaced on Moling's church.
My territory is downslope of a mountain breast
and the limestone cairns where the milk-white dead
lie in figurative simplicity of last ritual and appeasement.

Their breeding and attendant fevers are over.

My foraging heart sees to its horizon.

46.

Years it is, God, decades, since I last embraced fire.
I always associate flame with daring men,
Patricks that steal off the Trinity at Tara.

I would fan out my two wings to the tall flames
In the quaint manner of people with their hands
Hoping for the warming of my phantom limbs.

So great is my need for warmth, I'd settle
On a hollowed trunk near the fire you kindled.
Are we not all the reddest embers of each other?

Thinking like this, I wanted often to cry out my name
To you. My gizzard bulged with it. I kecked in silence.
But only the odd bird sound uttered that excited laughter

Which, thrown on the fire-talk started a little incandescence
In a sleep-gathering corner. I knew people must rise
To milk, child care at dawn, the tagging of herds,

Pray weekly under high windows to a fattening shepherd.
But, as I say, I've rarely ventured of late over to a fire
Content to wait withdrawn in your deepening shadows.

At home, in my prime, I loved the dawn rakings,
Nobody could light a fire the way I did.
It is a blessed thing to see great fires blazing on mountain tops.

Congregations wave to me every Bealtaine over Árd Éireann.
But I fly happier now close to the darkness of my days.
Voyager, light where pale ash accumulates.

47.

Emptiness.
In the skies
hear my soft location
note.

My plea,
like a lover's.
Void
over which I void

a future
generation,

the lit
haw

the tart
alder.

48.

My talons
grasp
at any
solitary
thorn.

Till
I
light
sway
in a
sloe

bush.

Beak
in the air.

49.

The grouse
stamps
its feet

vocalises
with its wings

no easy art

50.

Kingfisher
your body
is blue
dazzle,

melts
into the sunset
of a June
solstice.

Azure skies
on your feathers,

you
dress
rainbows
with hope.

51.

I'll dress
no more
in dolour
or colours.

Give me
mauves
golds
the warm purple.

Shards
of the sombre
I'd assembled
in my soul.

All miraculous
      plumage was
buried down a hole.

52.

Coming back to my home after all these years
I saw the green plain of Moira stretch below me
Its history and geography like leaves in October.

Familiar, on that showery day, the last roses
Trembling in sunlit benediction over doors.
I remember choosing for you a gift of blooms.

Yes, I was winging to that once cared for spot
I would care for too, without spade or hoe
With a swathe of colour and blustery sun.

My mother's grave lay in these warring fields.
Mother, surrogate mother, who fostered me.
I wed your grave with my beak in the sun.

I was winging off, my filial chore done,
When you called my name, said I'd not confessed
At all what I came for, I should tell all.

Then my plight tumbled out of me like a child.
It poured from me till my breast ached, I cried
My ills above where your warm hazel eyes lay

Though I could not see you for all the earth
Or read my fate in poems interred at your side.
My gormless captors made a rush at me.

But I took off to savour once more the great
Desolation of leafless spaces over Moira. Yet,
Off the ground I shook out in my whole frame.

A hunger came over me as never in my life
I could hardly hold myself aloft in the air,
Convulsed as if with some primal therapy.

Then I saw an orchard with reddened fruit
Lit down among the windfalls on the earth
Ate these as if breaking an old fast as a boy.

On that Armagh hill, each tree a russet galaxy,
I who had not eaten properly for decades
Devoured apple after apple. Beautiful apples!

Son. Mother. Your gaze was all about me.

53.

I cast off from my familiar perch in time
At the precise second of the first lauds bell
Up stream. As Moling would say, *Ad Originem.*

Trailing into the sun-red sky above the daffodil
Beds of March, I swung low out over the river
Crouched on the rock with a shag to take my fill.

I saw faces mimic me in the crystal water
Lose focus in the flow of year after year
Alan's, my own, your haggard chapter.

I heard religious sing up on the hill of man's degenerate nature
How through its brute necessities the world wears out
Christ comes to destroy old ways of behaviour.

O at Eastertide, in a week, or two, or thereabout.
And I remembered the consummate joy they sang of.
My heart hankered for that paradise they sang by rote.

Better than a mother's or lover's breast. What passed for love.
Then the horror of the depths of the river came over me.
A flower swept by me like a face to which I'd evolved.

I froze, then scattered upriver, abort in my own society;
Riverbank forest, slime depth and chapel held creatures
Who'd pick my bones and my soul in community.

It was not, at all, as if I spurned their natures
No, but neophyte again, with the light heart of the novice
I strove upriver from men and their bony structures

Harnessing horses in tillage, the seeds of business:
Upstream like sperm cast on a moist female thigh
As Moling set to the assorted chores of Genesis.

The curt wind opened up my breast keel in flight
The valley of the riverbed swallowed me whole.
In flesh and blood we wing on instinct in our plight.

Noon hid its light. March blew cloudy, primordial.
Dark with hail and sleet then a cold sleazy rain.
Daily, to the end, naked souls endure such ritual.

Till days grow warm, grow cold. The end of oxygen,
Blood and breath. Mother and child. My river narrows.
I enter the youthful womb of origins.

Up here its fenland, bog, oak stumps strewn in chaos.
Still, at a remove, the snow-capped hills. Up here the wind
Enjoys its forsaken pastures. The near absolute of loss.

I wheel about in all my mere lives with humankind,
In inhuman cries, until the heart burns
Up the purgatorial, the mad cycles, and I'm driven blind

With remorse like ice. The river erects to rivulet, learns
A sense of its beginning with that far timeless ocean,
The present. Stone is friable and in showers returns

Seaward by the melting streamlet. Mirroring the sun
Water disappears over the rockface, as if into thin air,
And I am lifted by an updraft, a great one

I did not reckon on. It takes my breath, this ether
And I am transported into a punishing blue space,
Hold, incinerate there the petty grind like a cancer.

Till reality hums, lights all things in their living embrace.
I sip on these tiny drafts of omniscience,
Realise in the mind's foetal warmth my own birthplace.

54.

I glide down from the height
        just as bereft as before.
The forced moult of the mountain
        leaves me bare.

Yet it was good
        to breast, above the beginning, the last rise
Chip at the speckled blue
        let in the timeless.

Hold onto time, with ridiculous talon, when time was not,
        if only for a blinding instant
When nothing was manifest in my features
        but their brightness.

And, so, I come down below white trailing cirrus
        and the home beyond home I barely knew.
Familiar tributaries
        conduct me to you.

Fields grow familiar.
    I know these people.
With creative reckoning
    Their wings, too, toil at clay.

I labour at last down onto Moling's Quay
    sink as exhausted there as any albatross.
Only the children hosanna about me.
    I feel their cool healing palms on my head.

My feather-torn follicles they dress with ointment.
    They spread out sweet fern where I stumble
And run exultant to where they'll hid me
    in a huddle of rushes I've made my own.

My feathers must bear some pigment
    of what I've seen.
That is why the children
    minister to me.

55.

I dream of a great love lifted up and the robe
That touched your skin, though ours be counterfeit.
Soldier at the cross, my handling of your clothes
Brought me peace. Now I'm lucky for the beat

Of your great oceans too. I can hold it more and more
In me, hear the controlled surges of tide and heart
Crashing with huge sudden combers on any shore.
And all of this is you, where our immersions start.

You are the deeper limes below me on the crests of waves.
The shallow's deep purples in the sunlight; that deeper blue,
The sky blue, our far mortal ancestors in high caves
Left in print with their warm hands as a salute to you.

In the skies, sometimes, I can breathe in on the essence
Of your love, grow strong from your oceanic tolerance.

56.

If you walk beneath midnight boughs of oak or beech,
You will hear the illusive wings of songbirds flutter
Beating in the dark. So, you may, too, sense me

Vacate, for fear of humans, the late branches I warmed
Fly deeper into our pre-birth, post-death state over land or water.
I think of the pursuers I leave now at my back,

My captors, with their cold blood-bright Moira hands
Sinking like giant bog reeds into November earth
Or reduced to redwings hugging dyke and river.

I grow tired of the conceited children of light.
There is no shadow of me that can't be thrown.
I have made companions of moonless moorlands.

Darkness is all, or nearly all, fills the halls of the universe.
Half our days are spent in it, when a good sleep beckons.
What is break of day but a digression into the temporary?

Our children spend their countless ten thousand years
Consigned to its benignity and soil, who only know
Sunlight for thirty, forty, fifty, sixty years, or less

Toil beneath the working noon. Pine for twilight.
All they have finally is darkness, gentle clay.
Much play is made of light in Moling's liturgy,

The Tara news with its Easter clichés.
What reflection has your sun on us out in the emptiness?
Our earth is but a lit-up grain in the infinite spaces.

I rest on the diaphragm of the dark, taste no fear,
Joy in my embrace of the wide-eyed field creatures
Reconnoitring morsels of pre-dawn sustenance,

Breathe in the scent of flowers that open out for us
With fragrance only at dusk, petal in their love at daybreak.
There are no good litanies to the dark, but there should be.

So, then, our seed-husk breaker of the buried wheat grain,
Enhancer of sleep, happy gloom of western hazel groves
Regenerator of Jesus in the rock, tenebrae of Samhain,

Black dove of the breeze, firmament with no stars,
The reassuring souls of cattle in dewy pre-oven pastures:
Best friend. Barn owl for brother, water bat for sister.

Fewer people are killed by night than in daylight.
Fact. Saviour of the universe, draw me into your darkness
Till I'm well kindled within your molten core.

I may believe yet in the green leaf that uncurls
The daffodil that opens, the apple unleashing its fragrance,
Open my wings at dawn for tomorrow's sunlit interlude.

57

Escaping the Hands of his Captors, Attempting a Hymn to Love

How fortunate those who have reaped your voice,
How fortunate those who have threshed your words,
How fortunate those who have stored your embrace,
How fortunate are they, they brim the wheaten throats of birds.

How fortunate are they who contemplate your hands.
How fortunate are they who kneel to massage your feet.
How fortunate are they who feed you on Galilee sands.
How fortunate those who sit next to your heartbeat.

How fortunate those who sink deep into your eyes,
How fortunate those who hug you in human flesh,
How fortunate those who watch you seed the nightly skies,
How fortunate are they who touch you above one closed eyelash.

How fortunate am I nightly now. I sleep by your tender side.
How fortunate, my wings thrown wide, and my young soul
      your bride.

58.

I fly as if into inward darkness, which is yet light, the eye
Of our vitreous humours, the greater consciousness.
A hollow sphere that is the one I am. All there is.

Accepting darkness made visible, I kindle a myth
Illuminating wings, ribcage and the keel.
I see with shining iris, but it is not mine.

59.

I touch, and am touched today, by affections.
Now all the old taboos are dead and gone
I fly higher in the air, cleanse my own name there.

I wing each day
up to the bleached scree
enter the bright concept before the waters.
Before any inkling on the blue mountain
     of the first spring.

Above the stormy clouds, azure weather
     is my element.

Back, down, then, to our human settlements.
Ramparts, hilltowns, clans, the mythic gibber of beaks.
Warmth of a sort, if territorial:

The sparrow hawk nest
in the fork of the branches,
maybe it's enough?

60.

Why bother about the decay of boughs
When there are other trees for home?

I skim the waters of the three sisters
Each river twice a week
Sunday take a breather
In the chapel of the shag on the rock
Reflect on the three in one
Creator, created, the affections
     we reciprocate.

Gardens I fly over, I do not know the gardener.
Trees planted in unison of time and space,
      I do not know the planter;
And the bare bleak summits where only scree holds good
      or not at all,
        the Architect of
          all this plenty.
I will never have exhausted the teeming valleys
Of praise and rebirth, the new year budding at leaf-fall.

61.

Whose plantations these are, I am not sure.
His village is perhaps over the rise
where the light dances in a suntrap
generations have made their home.

Then, up from the furze-beaten slope
'Carry me t'daddy' on my back,
the little wren.

As I wheel in the air
I remember
an incandescence of willow leaves in the sun
and seed, the down of seed, and many tendernesses
floating in the sunlit sky.
Like the artist, I had to drag myself out of the light
and into the rushes to capture the brightness
with startled eyes.

62.

On a sun-drenched afternoon of one mid-September
I took my ease near the river in Teach Moling
    through whose door
Fluff of the waterflower shone white in a passing galaxy
    all down the river.

Such a creation I would not have been witness
To were it not for the sun, had I not force rested,
Had not someone served me a kindly drink.

I have no resolution, today, but to seek out Eorann
Again, hopeless I know, my children's children
Whose nests are scattered, breathe peace toward the faces
    that hate me.

Fly until drop down to bleach my bones here
As good as anywhere as the poets declare.
What matters where one falls, supposing one knows how.
Any day I will depart from your mind's eye,
Graphic of a linnet foot in the pure snow.

63.

Syrinx makes voice in the sky
towards the humane
our cirrus home.

Harsh, if lofty.
A little
Perfection.

Across the mountains
      I wheel
       glen to glen
        giving

Praise

Praise

Praise

It is enough

Ethical Behavior in Early Childhood Education

Ethical Behavior in Early Childhood Education

by
Lilian G. Katz
Professor of Early Childhood Education
and
Director, ERIC Clearinghouse on
   Early Childhood Education
University of Illinois

and
Evangeline H. Ward
Professor of Early Childhood Education
Temple University

National Association for the Education of Young Children
Washington, D.C.

Photographs by

Ellen Levine Ebert 6, *10*
Jean Berlfein *23*
Steve Herzog *25*

Copyright © 1978. All rights reserved.
National Association for the Education of Young Children
1834 Connecticut Avenue, N.W.
Washington, DC 20009

Library of Congress Catalog Card Number: 78-57538
ISBN Catalog Number: 0-912674-61-X

Printed in the United States of America.

Contents

Foreword *J. D. Andrews*	vii
Ethical Issues in Working with Young Children *Lilian G. Katz*	1

What Do We Mean by a Code of Ethics?
Why Is a Code of Ethics Important?
What Are Some Examples of Ethical Problems?
What Next Steps Might Be Taken?

A Code of Ethics: The Hallmark of a Profession *Evangeline H. Ward*	17

For the Child
For the Parents and Family Members
For Myself and the Early Childhood Profession
For Administrators/Directors
For Policy/Decision Makers

*Children learn ethics
by our behavior and our attitudes
toward other people.*

Foreword

Edna Smith is not unusual. She has a temper that is much quicker and more consistent than is evident to people who don't know her well. She is an above average teacher in early childhood education. But like all of us, she may be unaware of how young children see her. Let's take a look at Edna in the classroom.

9:08. Johnny Brown is "given a talking to" because he will not share the tempera paints with Alice Green. Edna Smith uses this incident as an opportunity to talk to the group about "sharing with each other."

9:50. The teacher next door comes in and asks to borrow a book of songs. Edna politely refuses, indicating that she may be using the book later that morning. (The book is not used during the morning.)

1:20. Edna must leave her class for a few minutes to discuss a bill that she has been notified is unpaid. Edna is sure the check had been sent.

2:17. Linda Goldenburg stumbles over the block castle Tina Kowalski just built. Tina flies into a rage. Edna Smith talks to Tina about "forgive and forget."

3:15. Edna prepares to go to a meeting on ethics in early childhood education.

Don't think that Edna Smith is atypically hypocritical. If we search honestly, most of us, if not all, will find inconsistencies in our behavior—and personal ethics.

A child's eye is like a "candid camera." A child sees what we do, not merely what we say we do, and makes inferences and draws conclusions about ethical principles based on "real world" observations.

We adults tend not to see reality. We see self-images and other concepts. We can ignore the empirical evidence. We can rationalize.

A child often sees the truth more bluntly and nakedly than adults do and can very quickly detect the person who gives lip service to ethics but acts differently.

This is the problem with most discussions of ethics in early childhood education. *Ethics are something "out there." Ethics are dealt with as legal issues, abstract moral principles, and canons of professionalism.* They are impersonal concepts.

For young children, ethics are very personal. Rather than abstractions, ethics are inside people at the core of their being. Ethics are the genuine smile on your face, stopping to help the man whose car ran out of gas, treating the custodian like a human being, and cooperating with the teacher with whom you have a personality conflict. It is showing in your actions that you feel you are OK, and that other people are OK as well, worthy of respect and consideration.

This is the humanistic dimension of ethics. It is as important as it is neglected. Very few of us think about our responsibilities for dealing humanly with each other.

We who are involved in early childhood education should give more attention to the personal, humanistic dimension of ethics, for we ourselves are both the medium and the message of humanistic ethics. Children learn ethics by our behavior and our attitudes toward other people.

Therefore we need to exercise care about the behavioral model we present. Young children will see it like it is, and they will set their ethical standards accordingly.

J. D. Andrews
Washington, D.C.
June 1978

Ethical Issues in Working with Young Children
Lilian G. Katz

What should a teacher do when:

- a parent demands that she use a method of discipline that goes against her own preferences?
- the owner of his child care center appears to be giving false information to the licensing authorities?
- a parent complains to her about the behavior of a colleague?
- a child tells him about law breaking behavior observed at home?
- a mother pours out all her personal troubles?

The list of questions of this kind is potentially very long. But answers to such questions cannot be drawn from research reports, from the accumulated knowledge of child development, or even from educational philosophy. The issues raised and their answers lie in the realm of professional ethics.

One of the characteristic features of a profession is that its practitioners share a code of ethics, usually developed, promoted, and monitored by a professional society or association. Agreement on whether an occupation is really a bona fide profession, or when it becomes so, is difficult to obtain (Becker 1962). In this chapter the term *profession* is used in its general sense to refer to an occupation that is client-service centered as distinguished from those occupations that are profit or product centered or bureaucratically organized. While early childhood workers are not yet professionalized, their work frequently gives rise to the kinds of problems addressed by codes of ethics.

The purpose of this chapter is to encourage discussion of the complex ethical problems encountered by early childhood workers. I shall attempt to suggest some of the central issues by addressing the following questions:

What do we mean by a code of ethics?

Why is a code of ethics important?

What are some examples of ethical conflicts in day care and preschool work?

What steps might be taken to help early childhood workers resolve these conflicts?

What Do We Mean by a Code of Ethics?

Of all the dictionary definitions of *ethics* available, the one most relevant here is "the system or code of morals of a particular philosopher, religion, group, profession, etc."* More specifically, Moore defines *ethics* as " . . . private systems of law which are characteristic of all formally constituted organizations" (1970, p. 116). He notes also that these codes " . . . highlight proper relations with clients or others outside the organizations, rather than procedural rules for organizational behavior" (p. 116). Similarly, Bersoff says that ethics " . . . refer to the way a group of associates defines their special responsibility to one another and the rest of the social order in which they work" (1975, p. 359).

Levine (1972), in his examination of the complex ethical problems that arise in the practice of psychiatry, proposes that codes of ethics can be understood as one of the methods by which groups of workers cope with their temptations. He suggests also that ethics have

---

Webster's Unabridged, 2nd ed., s.v. "ethics."

Ethical Issues

the function of minimizing the distorting effects of wishful thinking, of limiting or inhibiting one's destructive impulses. In addition, Levine asserts that codes of ethics embody those principles or forces which stand in opposition to self-aggrandizement—especially when self-aggrandizement might be at the expense of others. Similarly, according to Levine, ethics provide guidelines for action in cases of potentially significant damage to others, or potential harm to another's interests.

In much the same spirit, Eisenberg (1975) proposes a "general law that the more powerful a change agent, or a given treatment, the riskier its application" (p. 102). As the risk to either the client or the practitioner increases, the necessity for ethical guidelines seems to increase.

From time to time, I have asked students in early childhood education to try to develop codes of ethics for themselves. Invariably they produce sets of statements that are more appropriately defined as "goals" rather than ethics, although the distinctions between the two are not always easily made. The statement, "I shall impart knowledge and skills," seems to belong to the category of goals. The statement, "I shall respect the child's ethnic background," more easily seems to belong to the category of ethics. The major distinction between the two categories seems to be that goals are broad statements about the effects one intends to have. Ethics, on the other hand, seem to be statements about how to conduct oneself in the course of implementing goals.

In summary, a *code of ethics* may be defined as a *set of statements that helps us to deal with the temptations inherent in our occupations.* A code of ethics may also help us to act in terms of that which we believe to be right rather than what is expedient—especially when doing what we believe is right carries risks. Situations in which doing what is right carries high probability of getting an award or being rewarded may not require a code of ethics as much as situations rife with risks (e.g., risking the loss of a job or a license to practice, facing professional alienation or even harsher consequences). Codes of ethics are statements about right or good ways to conduct ourselves in the course of implementing our goals. They are statements that *en*courage us (i.e., give us the courage) to act in accordance with our professional judgment of what is best for the clients being served even when they may not agree. Codes of ethics give us courage to act in terms of what we believe to be in the best interests of the client rather than in terms of what will make our clients like us. Needless to say, the ethical principles implied in the code reflect the group's position on what is valuable and worthwhile in society in general.

For the purposes of this chapter, the main features of codes of ethics considered are the group's beliefs about:
- what is right rather than expedient,
- what is good rather than simply practical,
- what acts members must never engage in or condone even if those acts would *work* or if members *could get away with* such acts, acts to which they must never be accomplices, bystanders, or contributors.

Why Is a Code of Ethics Important?

The specific aspects of working with preschool children that give rise to ethical problems addressed here are the (1) power and status of practitioners, (2) multiplicity of clients, (3) ambiguity of the data base, and (4) role ambiguity. Each aspect is discussed below.

Power and Status of Practitioners

In any profession, the more powerless the client is in relation to the practitioner, the more important the practitioner's ethics become. That is to say, the greater the power of the practitioner over the client, the greater the necessity for internalized restraints against abusing that power.

Early childhood practitioners have great power over young children, especially in day care centers. Practitioners' superior physical power over young children is obvious. In addition, practitioners have virtually total power over the psychological *goods and resources* of value to the young in their care. The young child's power to modify a teacher's behavior is largely dependent on the extent to which a teacher yields that power to the child. Whatever power children might have over their caregivers' behavior is unlikely to be under conscious control. Obviously young children cannot effectively organize strikes or boycotts or report malpractice to the authorities. Children may report to a parent what they perceive to be abusive caregiver behavior, but the validity of such reports is often questionable. Furthermore, parental reactions to these reports may be unreliable. In one case, a five-year-old reported to his mother that he had been given only one slice of bread during the day at the center as punishment for misbehavior. His mother was reported to have responded by saying, "Then tomorrow, behave yourself."

It is neither possible nor desirable to monitor teachers constantly in order to ensure that such abuses do not occur. Since there are often no "other experts watching," as Moore (1970) puts it, and the child's self-protective repertoire is limited, a code of ethics, internalized as commitments to *right* conduct, might help to strengthen resistance to occupational temptations and help practitioners make ethical choices.

Another aspect of the work of early childhood practitioners that affects ethical behavior is the relatively low status of practitioners in the early childhood field. Parents seem far more likely to make demands on practitioners for given kinds of practices in preschool and child care centers than they are to demand specific medical procedures from pediatricians, for example.

An example is an incident involving a young mother who brought her four-year-old son to the day care center every morning at 7:30 and picked him up again every evening around 5:30 p.m. She gave the staff strict instructions that under no circumstances was the child to nap during the day. She explained that when she took her son home in the evenings, she was tired from her long day and needed to be able to feed him and have him tucked away for the night as soon as possible. It is not difficult to picture the difficulties encountered by the staff of this proprietary day care center. By the middle of the afternoon this child was unmanageable.

The state regulations under which the center was licensed specified a daily rest period for all children. Sensitivity and responsiveness to parental preferences, however, were also main tenets of the center's philosophy. Although the staff attempted to talk to the mother about the child's fatigue and intractability, the mother had little regard for the staff's expertise and judgment, and total disregard for state licensing standards.

In this situation, the staff was frustrated and angered by the mother and the child, and felt victimized by both. Could they put the child down for a nap and get away with it? A real temptation! Would that work? Would it be right? It might have been right to ask the mother to place her child in a different center. But such a suggestion has risks: A proprietary day care center is financially dependent on maintaining as full enrollment as possible. Also, in some communities, alternative placements are simply not available.

Accumulated experience suggests that four-year-old children thrive best with adequate rest periods during the day, and a state regulation requiring such a program provision is unlikely to be controversial. The problem outlined above could have been solved by invoking the state's regulations. But state regulations are not uniformly observed! Why should this particular one be honored and others overlooked?

Working daily with young and relatively powerless clients is likely to carry with it many temptations to abuse that power. Practitioners may have been tempted at one time or another to regiment the children, treat them all alike, intimidate them into conformity to adult demands, reject unattractive children, or become deeply attached to some children. Thus the hortatory literature addressed to early childhood practitioners reminds them to respect individual differences, accept children, use positive guidance, and treat children with dignity. It seems reasonable to suggest that most such exhortations should be part of a code of ethics.

Multiplicity of Clients

A code of ethics may help practitioners resolve issues arising from the fact that they serve a variety of client groups. Most early childhood workers, when asked, "Who is your client?" usually respond without hesitation, "The child." But it is probably more realistic to order the client groups into a hierarchy so that parents are the primary group (see Bersoff 1975), children secondary, the employing agency and the larger community next (see also Beker 1976). Each group of clients in the hierarchy may be perceived as exerting pressures for practitioners to act in ways that may be against the

Working daily with young and relatively powerless clients is likely to carry with it many temptations to abuse that power.

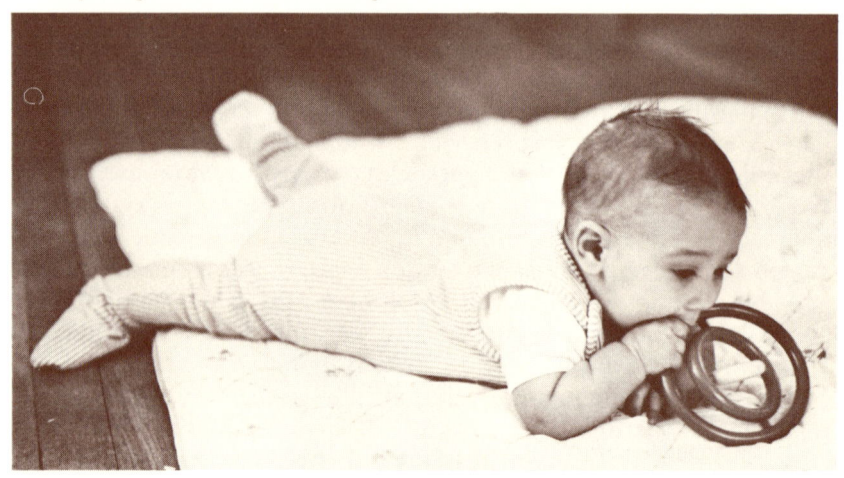

Ethical Issues

best interests of another client group. As a case in point, early childhood workers often lament the fact that many parents want their preschoolers to learn to read, while they themselves consider such instruction premature and therefore potentially harmful to the children. At times, the best interests of both parents and children may be in conflict with agency interests and expectations, and so forth. A code of ethics should help to clarify the position of each client group in the hierarchy, and provide guidelines on how to resolve questions concerning which of the groups has the best claim to practitioners' consideration.

Ambiguity of the Data Base

Many differences of opinion on courses of action cannot be resolved by reference to either state/local regulations or a reliable body of evidence. Weakness in the data base of a professional field often causes a vacuum that is likely to be filled by ideologies. The field of early childhood education is one that seems to qualify as ideology-bound (see Katz 1975), giving rise to a variety of temptations for practitioners. The uncertainty and/or unavailability of reliable empirical findings about the long-term developmental consequences of early experiences tempts practitioners (as well as their leaders) to develop orthodoxies and become doctrinaire in their collective statements. Such orthodoxies and doctrines may be functional to the extent that they provide practitioners with a sense of conviction and the confidence necessary for action. Such conviction, however, may be accompanied by rejection of alternative methods and of some of the facts that may be available. A code of ethics could serve to remind practitioners to eschew orthodoxies, strive to be well-informed and open-minded, and keep abreast of new ideas and developments.

Role Ambiguity

Research and development activities of recent years have resulted in emphasis on the importance of the developmental and stimulus functions of early childhood practitioners as compared with more traditional custodial and guidance functions. In addition, recent policies related to early childhood emphasize parental involvement on all levels of programming, concern for nutrition and health screening, and relevant social services. These pressures and policies add to and aggravate a longstanding problem of role ambiguity for early childhood workers.

The central source of ambiguity stems from the general proposition that the younger the child served, the wider the range of his or her functioning for which adults must assume responsibility. Early childhood practitioners cannot limit their concerns only to children's academic progress and *pupil role* socialization. The immaturity of the client presses the practitioner into responding to almost all of the child's needs and behavior. Responsibility for the *whole child* may lead to uncertainty over role boundaries, for example, in cases of disagreement with parents over methods of discipline, toilet-training, sex role socialization, and so on. Clarification of the boundaries of practitioner roles and/or the limits of their expertise could be reflected in a code of ethics.

In summary, four aspects of the role of early childhood workers seem to imply the necessity for a code of ethics: high power and low status, multiplicity of client groups, and ambiguity in the data base and in the role boundaries of practitioners. It seems reasonable to suggest that the actual problems encountered by practitioners in the course of daily practice typically reflect combinations of several of these aspects.

What Are Some Examples of Ethical Problems?

Some examples of situations that seem to call upon early childhood practitioners to make ethical choices are outlined below. The examples are discussed in terms of relationship with major client groups such as parents, children, colleagues, and employers.

Ethical Issues Involving Parents

Perhaps the most persistent ethical problems faced by early childhood practitioners are those encountered in their relations with parents. One common source of problems stems from the fact that practitioners generally reflect and cherish middle-class values and tend to confuse conventional behavior with normal development. The recent increase in practitioners' self-consciousness about being middle class seems to have increased their hesitancy to take a stand in controversies with parents.

Within any given group of parents, preferences and values may vary widely according to the parents' membership in particular cultural, ethnic, or socioeconomic groups. A practitioner may, for example, choose to reinforce children as they develop conventional

Ethical Issues

sex role stereotypes. But one or more parents in the client group may prefer what has come to be called an "alternative lifestyle." Or a parent may demand of his child's caregiver that his son not be allowed to play with dolls, even though the caregiver may prefer not to discourage such play.

When practitioners are committed to respect and respond to parental values and input, they may be faced with having to choose between what is right and what is right. What data of pedagogical principles can be brought to bear on such choices?

Similar types of parent-staff ethical conflicts arise from discrepancies between parental and practitioner preferences with respect to curriculum goals and methods. For example, practitioners often prefer informal, open, or child-centered curriculum goals and methods, while parents opt for traditional methods. If parents are the primary clients of the staff, what posture should the staff take when discrepancies in preferences occur?

Specifically, suppose a child in an informal setting produces art work that appears to her parents to be nothing more than scribbles. On the other hand, the caregiver respects the work as the child's attempts at self-expression and also values the kinds of fine motor skill development such a product supports. Suppose further that the practitioner knows the art work might cause a parent to make demeaning remarks to the child, or even scold her. Suppose the same caregiver also knows that if the child brings home work regarded by the parents as evidence that the child is mastering the "Three R's," her parents would compliment and reward her. How should the caregiver resolve the conflict between her pedagogical preferences and the demands of the home on the child? What choice would be in the best interests of the child? It is unlikely that such issues can be settled on the basis of available evidence (see Spodek 1977a).

Disagreements between practitioners and parents as to which child behaviors should be permitted, modified, or punished are legion. Some of the disagreements are a function of differences between the referent baselines of the two groups. Practitioners tend to assess and evaluate behavior against a baseline derived from experience with hundreds of children in the age group concerned. Thus their concepts of what is the normal or typical range of behavior for the age group are apt to be much wider than parents' concepts. As a result, practitioners' tolerance for children's behaviors such as thumb-sucking, crying, masturbation, using dirty words, aggression, sexual and sex role experimentation, etc., is likely to be greater than that of the majority of parents. Parents do not universally accept the wisdom that comes from practitioners' experience, and not infrequently instruct them to prohibit what practitioners themselves accept as normal behavior. How can practitioners respect parental preferences and their own expertise as well?

In the course of their daily work, preschool practitioners often encounter a mother or father who involves them in their total life problems. For example, a mother may spill out all her personal problems to her child's preschool teacher. In such a case, the practitioner may find herself with unwelcome information.

Two kinds of ethical issues emerge from such cases. First, the parent may be seeking advice on matters that lie outside the practitioner's training and expertise. As a result the practitioner may want to refer the parent to specialized counseling or treatment. Are there risks in making such referrals? What about the possibility that the unwanted information implies to the practitioner that the child might be in psychological danger, and the mother rejects the recommendation for specialized help?

The daily work of early childhood practitioners is fraught with ambiguities. A code of ethics may help practitioners cope with the ambiguities with greater success.

Ethical Issues

Ethically, what are the limits of the practitioner's responsibility to the *whole child?* Secondly, such cases are representative of many other occupational situations that require confidentiality and sensitivity in handling information about clients' private lives. A code of ethics should address issues concerning the limits of expertise and the confidentiality of information.

Another example of ethical issues in practitioner-parent relations concerns the risks and limits of truthfulness in sharing information with parents and colleagues. For example, parents often ask caregivers and early childhood teachers about their children's behavior. In some cases, a parent wants to check up on his/her child in order to learn whether the child is persisting in undesirable behavior. If the practitioner knows that a truthful report will lead to severe punishment of the child, how should she reply? Similarly, in filling out reports on children's progress for use by others, practitioners often worry about whether a truthful portrayal of a given child will result in prejudicial and damaging treatment by practitioners in the setting receiving the report. Withholding information is a type of playing God that causes considerable anxiety in teachers generally.

In a similar way, let us suppose that a practitioner had good reason to believe that making a positive report to a parent about a child's behavior (even though the report might be untrue or exaggerated) would improve relations between the child and his parents. Even if the ploy had a high probability of working, would it be ethically defensible?

In summary, early childhood practitioners face constant ethical dilemmas in their relations with parents. Contemporary emphasis on greater involvement and participation of parents in their children's education and care is likely to increase and intensify these problems. A code of ethics cannot solve the problem encountered by preschool practitioners. But it can provide a basis upon which staff members and their clients could, together, confront and think through their common and separate responsibilities, concerns, and ideas about what they believe to be right.

Ethical Issues Involving Children

One of the sources of ethical conflicts for preschool workers stems from the fact that the young child has not yet been socialized into the role of pupil. A ten-year-old has been socialized to know very well that some things are not discussed with teachers at school. The preschooler does not yet have a sense of the boundaries between home and school, and what one should or should not tell caregivers and teachers. Children often report information about activities that practitioners would rather not have. For instance, children sometimes report on illegal or private activities going on at home. For one thing, the reliability of the report is difficult to assess. For another, asking leading follow-up questions may encourage a child to *tell too much*. What should a practitioner do with such information? Practitioners sometimes find themselves at a loss for words in such situations (Rosenberg and Ehrgott 1977).

Another type of problem related to program activities seems to have ethical implications. Children's enjoyment of certain activities should of course be considered in program planning, but this attribute of an activity is not sufficient in and of itself to justify its inclusion in a program. For example, children like to watch television but are not adequate judges of what programs are worthwhile. This type of problem involves complex pedagogical, psychological, and ethical issues (see Peters 1966). Sometimes such problems are confounded by caregivers' tendencies to be motivated by a strong wish to be loved, accepted, or appreciated by the children. Children's affection and respect for caregivers and early childhood teachers is one useful indicator of their effectiveness. But such positive child responses should be consequences of right action rather than motives underlying practitioners' choices and decisions.

Preschool practitioners are increasingly under pressure to teach children academic skills. On the whole, practitioners appear to resist such pressures, not only on the basis of the possible prematurity of such skill learning, but also as part of a general rejection of structured or traditional schooling. Occasionally, however, the pressure may be so great as to tempt practitioners into giving their charges crash courses on test items, thereby minimizing the likelihood of a poor showing on standardized tests.

Even if practitioners can get away with such tactics, should they be ethically constrained against doing so? Should a code of ethics address questions of what stand to take on the uses and potential abuses of tests for assessing achievement, for screening, and for labeling children?

Ethical Issues Involving Colleagues and Employing Agencies

One of the most common sources of conflict between coworkers in early childhood settings centers around divergent views on how to treat children. Staff meetings conducted by supervisors, or supervisory intervention and assistance on a one-to-one basis, seem to be the appropriate strategies for resolving such conflicts. But when a parent complains to one teacher about another, how should the recipient of the complaint respond? Such cases often offer a real temptation to side with the complainant. But would that response be right?

Perhaps one guideline that may be relevant to such interstaff conflicts would be for the individual practitioners involved to ask themselves (and other appropriate resource people) whether the objectionable practice is really harmful to children. If the answer, after serious reflection, is clearly "Yes," then action by the appropriate authority must be taken to stop the harmful practice. But the state of the art of early childhood education does not yet lend itself to definitive answers to all questions of *clear and present danger* to children. If the practices in question are objectionable merely on the grounds of taste, ideological persuasion, or orthodoxy, then practitioners should resist the temptation to indulge in feuds among themselves and alliances with parents against each other.

Examples of ethical dilemmas facing practitioners in their relations with employers include those in which practitioners are aware of violations of state or local regulations, misrepresentations of operating procedures in reports to licensing authorities, or instances of an owner's misrepresentation of the nature of the program and services offered to clients. To what extent should practitioners contribute, even passively, to such violations? Most early childhood personnel work without contracts, and thus risk losing their jobs if they give evidence or information that might threaten the operating license of their employing agency. Should employees be silent bystanders in these kinds of situations? Silence would be practical, but would it be ethical?

Another type of dilemma confronts practitioners when agencies providing day care services require declarations of income from parents in order to determine their fees. One such case concerned a welfare mother who finally obtained a job and realized that the day care fees corresponding to her income would cause her actual income to amount to only a few more dollars than she had been receiving on welfare. Yet she really wanted to work. Her child's caregiver advised her not to tell the agency that she was employed and wait for the authorities to bring up the matter first. It is easy to see that the practitioner in this situation was an active agent in violating agency and state regulations. But she also knew that alternative arrangements for child care were unavailable to this mother, and that the child had just begun to feel at home and to thrive in the day care center. The practitioner judged the whole family's best interests to be undermined by the income-fee regulations. How could a code of ethics address such an issue?

What Next Steps Might Be Taken?

Some preliminary steps toward developing a code of ethics have already been taken. The Minnesota Association for the Education of Young Children (MnAEYC) adopted a *Code of Ethical Conduct Responsibilities* in 1976 (MnAEYC 1976). The code enumerates a total of thirty-four principles divided into three categories: (1) General Principles for All Members, (2) Additional Principles for Members Who Serve Children in a Specific Capacity, and (3) Members Who Serve Through Ancillary Services such as Training, Licensing, etc. The third category contains nineteen principles and is further delineated into four subcategories for members who are trainers, licensing personnel, parents, and supervisors and administrators.

Many of the principles listed in the MnAEYC Code correspond to suggestions made in this chapter. A number of the principles, however, might be more applicable to job descriptions than to a code of ethics (e.g., Principle 29 for Supervisors states, " . . . should provide regular in-service training to further staff development and to meet licensing requirements when appropriate"). Three of the principles are addressed to members who are parents. Because parents are clients rather than practitioners, the appropriateness of including them in a practitioners' code of ethics is doubtful.

An initial code of ethics for early childhood education and development professionals is proposed by Ward in the following chapter. These statements cover a wide range of aspects of working with young children and, together with the code adopted by MnAEYC, could provide a useful basis for further discussion.

It seems advisable to begin at a local level to refine these codes or develop another code. Small groups of workers at a given day care or child development center or locale might constitute themselves into an ethics committee and thrash through issues to determine where they stand. Local efforts and problems could be shared with ethics committees of statewide associations.

The process of developing and refining a code of ethics will undoubtedly be slow and arduous. Many practitioners are cynical about the value of such codes. But, as Levine (1972) points out, the work of developing a code involves self-scrutiny, which in and of itself may strengthen resistance to the many temptations encountered in practice. Furthermore, recent research on helping behavior suggests that individuals' responses to their own conflicting impulses are strongly influenced by their perceptions of the norms of the group with whom they identify (see Wilson 1976). The norms of our colleague group, articulated in a code of ethics, may help to give us the feeling that colleagues will back us if we take a risky (but courageous) stand, or censure us if we fail to live up to the code. The daily work of early childhood practitioners is fraught with ambiguities. A code of ethics may help practitioners cope with the ambiguities with greater success.

* * *

The material in this chapter was prepared pursuant to a contract with the National Institute of Education, U.S. Department of Health, Education, and Welfare. Contractors undertaking such projects under government sponsorship are encouraged to express freely their judgment in professional and technical matters. Prior to publication, the manuscript was submitted to the Area Committee for Early Childhood Education at the University of Illinois for critical review and determination of professional competence. This publication has met such standards. Points of view or opinions, however, do not necessarily represent the official view or opinions of either the Area Committee or the National Institute of Education.

References

Becker, H. S. "The Nature of a Profession." In *Education for the Professor*, ed. N. B. Henry. The Sixty-First Yearbook of the National Society for the Study of Education. Chicago: University of Chicago Press, 1962.
Beker, J. "On Defining the Child Care Profession—I." *Child Care Quarterly* 5, no. 3 (Fall 1976): 165-166.
Bersoff, D. N. "Professional Ethics and Legal Responsibilities: On the Horns of a Dilemma." *Journal of School Psychology* 13, no. 4 (1975): 359-376.
Eisenberg, L. "The Ethics of Intervention: Acting Amidst Ambiguity." *Journal of Child Psychiatry* 16, no. 2 (April 1975): 93-104.
Katz, L. G. "Early Childhood Education and Ideological Disputes." *Educational Forum* 3, no. 39 (March 1975): 267-271.
Katz, L. G. *Talks with Teachers.* Washington, D.C.: National Association for the Education of Young Children, 1977.
Levine, M. *Psychiatry and Ethics.* New York: George Braziller, 1972.
Minnesota Association for the Education of Young Children. *Code of Ethical Responsibilities.* 1976. MnAEYC, 1821 University Ave., Rm. 373, S. St. Paul, MN 55104.
Moore, W. E. *The Professions: Roles and Roles.* New York: Russell Sage Foundation, 1970.

Peters, R. S. *Ethics and Education.* Glenview, Ill.: Scott, Foresman & Co., 1966.
Rosenberg, H., and Ehrgott, R. H. "Games Teachers Play." *School Review* 85, no. 3 (May 1977): 433-437.
Spodek, B. "Curriculum Construction in Early Childhood Education." In *Early Childhood Education,* ed. B. Spodek and H. J. Walberg. Berkeley, Calif.: McCutchan, 1977a.
Spodek, B. "From the President." *Young Children* 32, no. 4 (May 1977b): 2-3.
Wilson, J. P. "Motivation, Modeling, and Altruism: A Person x Situation Analysis." *Journal of Personality and Social Psychology* 34, no. 6 (December 1976): 1078-1086.

A Code of Ethics: The Hallmark of a Profession
Evangeline H. Ward

It is customary, when a profession elects to develop a code of ethics, to prepare a draft and extend to its members the opportunity for reactions, criticisms, additions, or deletions. To my knowledge, the early childhood education and development profession has no such code. On two occasions in 1976, an exploration of ethics in early childhood education was undertaken (Delaware Valley Association for the Education of Young Children conference in Philadelphia and the Bicentennial Conference on Early Childhood Education at the University of Miami). Coincidentally, one of the sessions at the fiftieth anniversary conference of the National Association for the Education of Young Children in that same year was devoted to ethical issues in working with young children. Especially since August 1974, the nation has focused its concern on the lines distinguishing ethical from nonethical behavior at all levels of society. This chapter represents an effort to extend this inquiry toward the development of a code of ethics for our profession.

The National Association for the Education of Young Children is a distinguished organization in the forefront of leadership in the education and care of young children. It would be appropriate for NAEYC to assume leadership in this as-yet-uncharted area of ethics for the field of early childhood education. This association develops

---

Portions of this chapter are reprinted from *Teaching Practices: Reexamining Assumptions*, edited by B. Spodek. Washington, D.C.: National Association for the Education of Young Children, 1977.

services to its 30,000 members that encourage planned progress toward improved conditions for young children and their families. Thus, it consciously supports values in the direction of accountability for practices that are defensible in terms of what is known in early education. This is an ethical and moral responsibility as well as one mandated by its incorporation. It is indeed movement toward professionalism.

> Each profession has its own history, its unique problems, its own forms of training, its own heroes and villains, its own way of policing itself. Each of them today is caught in something like an identity crisis. But all of them share with the larger society something of the anguish of the moral crisis of our time. Each profession has codes of ethics listing its standards. How I behave in the face of these codes characterizes me as a conscious professional. . . . A member of a profession is someone who is educated and trained for it and presumably skilled in it, who takes it seriously and is somehow (not always well) remunerated for it and who gives it major attention and submits the results to the scrutiny of professional colleagues and the larger world. (Lerner 1975, p. 10)
>
> Compared with morality in other areas—politics, business, or law, for example, education's condition seems admirable. . . . To say that education's ethics compare favorably with those of other aspects of contemporary America, however, is not sufficient reason to give it a passing grade. (Hechinger 1975, p. 27)
>
> The teacher will be required to be scrupulously professional and ethical in his treatment of individuals and in the exercise of his influence. (Houston and Howsam 1972, p. 15)

A Code of Ethics

If we agree with Lerner (1975) that each profession should have a code of ethics commensurate with its standard-setting role, then a beginning for setting standards and for identifying an appropriate ethical stance is in order for NAEYC.

Those engaged in providing educational, developmental, and caring services to young children and their families in today's complex living-learning-growing settings regularly face many dilemmas. Often more questions than answers are available. How would you, as an early childhood practitioner, respond to these situations?

- What is your ethical responsibility or stance when "just one more child" is added to a group? What motivates your response? *Is it really to know and help one more child grow to his or her full capacities or are other motives involved?*
- Do you really believe that parents and family members are the single most important continuing influencers of a child's educational and learning style? *What do you do to help parents and families use the services you can offer on behalf of their child?* What, in good ethical practice, indicates this role in action?
- Do you know about the alternative approaches to early childhood education and the range of curricula available in addition to the one you use in your program or center? Is it ever ethical to assume that every group of children or every individual child can develop best with exposure to a single approach? Since children grow (and change) and what we know about this growth is complex, what is the justification for approaching their development from a single point of view? *Do you select from many approaches to reach each child in order to accommodate idiosyncrasies of growth and change?*

The members of a profession monitor themselves from within. They take appropriate steps to ensure the ethical bases of programs, goals, and directions. They critique themselves, monitor their public image, and take the necessary risks to improve themselves and their field. If we are further to establish ourselves as professionals, we must set high ethical and professional standards by creating conditions for the protection of children, their families, and the profession. We must strengthen established principles and remain true to commitments to young children and their families and to their future lives in this country.

A code of ethics must be established. The following is a beginning step with three primary commitments: (1) to each child as an individual; (2) to each family as a unique constellation of people; and

(3) to oneself and the profession. A given in this is that those who assist in the professionalization of a field bring their individual values, codes of conduct and character as individuals, to the process.

An Initial Code of Ethics for Early Childhood Educators

Preamble

As an educator of young children in their years of greatest vulnerability, I, to the best of intent and ability, shall devote myself to the following commitments and act to support them.

For the Child

I shall accord the respect due each child as a human being from birth on.

I shall recognize the unique potentials to be fulfilled within each child.

I shall provide access to differing opinions and views inherent in every person, subject, or thing encountered as the child grows.

I shall recognize the child's right to ask questions about the unknowns that exist in the present so the answers (which may be within the child's capacity to discover) may be forthcoming eventually.

I shall protect and extend the child's physical well-being, emotional stability, mental capacities, and social acceptability.

For the Parents and Family Members

I shall accord each child's parents and family members respect for the responsibilities they carry.

By no deliberate action on my part will the child be held accountable for the incidental meeting of his or her parents and the attendant lodging of the child's destiny with relatives and siblings.

Recognizing the continuing nature of familial strength as support for the growing child, I shall maintain objectivity with regard to what I perceive as family weaknesses.

Maintaining family value systems and pride in cultural-ethnic choices or variations will supersede any attempts I might inadvertently or otherwise make to impose my values.

Because advocacy on behalf of children always requires that someone cares about or is strongly motivated by a sense of fairness and intervenes on behalf of children in relation to those services and institutions that impinge on their lives, I shall support family strength.

For Myself and the Early Childhood Profession

Admitting my biases is the first evidence of my willingness to become a conscious professional.

Knowing my capacity to continue to learn throughout life, I shall vigorously pursue knowledge about contemporary developments in early education by informal and formal means.

My role with young children demands an awareness of new knowledge that emerges from varied disciplines and the responsibility to use such knowledge.

Recognizing the limitation I bring to knowing intimately the ethical-cultural value systems of the multicultural American way of life, I shall actively seek the understanding and acceptance of the chosen ways of others to assist them educationally in meeting each child's needs for his or her unknown future impact on society.

Working with other adults and parents to maximize my strengths and theirs, both personally and professionally, I shall provide a model to demonstrate to young children how adults can create an improved way of living and learning through planned cooperation.

The encouragement of language development with young children will never exceed the boundaries of propriety or violate the confidence and trust of a child or that child's family.

I shall share my professional skills, information, and talents to enhance early education for young children wherever they are.

I shall cooperate with other persons and organizations to promote programs for children and families that improve their opportunities to utilize and enhance their uniqueness and strength.

I shall ensure that individually different styles of learning are meshed compatibly with individually different styles of teaching to help all people grow and learn well—this applies to adults learning to be teachers as well as to children.

Reprise: The Continuation of a Code

The perspective of those who teach young children generated the above code. Included in the early childhood education, development, and care profession are also those whose influence and different perspectives impinge importantly on the ethical behaviors of teachers and other staff personnel: (1) administrators/directors and (2) policy/decision makers. In the first group are those with direct responsibility for onsite management and supervision of program services; in the second group are those who are powerful influences but who function in less direct ways affecting both quality and quantity of services to families and children (volunteer boards, councils, religious bodies, proprietors, and governmental representatives).

This extension of a developing code of ethics focuses on these members of the profession. They differ specifically by reason of the delicate immediate choices required in face-to-face situations with peers, parents, and children on a daily basis. Directors are often unable to await patterned or accumulated evidence before action or decisions are required involving ethics. On the contrary, policy/decision makers may cogitate and discuss in groups the ethics of policies without this direct face-off. Additionally, time and distance stand between them and program operations. Though one might speculate on or wish for a narrowing of these, the facts are that there are, at best, intermittent contacts between those who define the broad policies within which programs must operate and those staff, families, and children experiencing the services. A code of ethics is incomplete unless it addresses these members and their commitments.

For Administrators/Directors

In view of the major responsibilities I carry for the total program of services in early education, care, and development, it is ethically sound to fulfill the following commitments:

I shall maintain the program by the highest known standards as if my own children were being served.

I shall base the continuation of a program only on documented evidence that the community, its families, and children can be qualitatively served in the clearly defined ways promised—or arrange for its orderly dissolution.

I shall make information about services of the program openly and accurately available, since the general public has more than a

Those engaged in providing services to young children and their families regularly face many dilemmas. Often more questions than answers are available.

casual concern for their young children—in the present as well as in the future.

I shall provide for open access to the program while maintaining essential safeguards for the privacy of individual children and their families and, at the same time, respect their legal rights to freedom of the information gained as their children grow and learn within the provisions of the program.

I shall establish and maintain systematic procedures to record what the program offers and why, how the services function, and how they can be improved and/or expanded to provide quality education and care.

I shall document to the appropriate policy/decision-making bodies the need for improvement, suggest areas in which existing limitations need to be eliminated, and propose appropriate changes.

I shall keep abreast of current and projected developments in the field that may serve to be advantageous or disadvantageous to present directions and operations.

I shall respect each staff member as a person, family member, and contributing professional whose job well done is vital to program success.

I shall engage staff in cooperative problem solving, planning, and continuing evaluation of both themselves and the program.

I shall evaluate and release staff if parents, family members, and the community cannot be assured that they are equal to sensitive handling and respect for the "educability" of the children, and knowledgeable of the necessity to share the children's educational and developmental progress witnessed in the program in planned communications.

I shall ensure adequate compensation for those employed in programs, including benefits related to personal and professional leave, hospitalization and illness protection, unemployment insurance, etc.

I shall provide professional advancement opportunities for myself and staff through in-service programs and external resources (literature, media, workshops, consultants, conferences).

I shall be fiscally accountable for services rendered commensurate with the stated goals and directions without sacrificing quality for quantity of service.

I shall implement regulations that govern programs for young children acknowledging that local, state, and federal efforts to protect children are, at best, minimal and are established not only as goals to be reached but as standards below which children are vulnerable and susceptible to damage.

For Policy/Decision Makers

In view of my voluntary selection or election to serve as a decision maker on behalf of families and children in agencies and institutions, I shall function to the best of my knowledge and abilities as a person who values these ethical practices.

I shall admit that my contributions can make a difference in the professionalization of services to young children and their families.

I shall serve in a citizen's capacity (generally without financial compensation) to promote and protect children and families from unscrupulous practices endorsed in the name of public service regardless of program sponsorship.

I shall draw heavily on the ideas and opinions of parents, community leaders, early education workers, and specialists in related fields and agencies in the formulation of my stance on decisions. This assures attention to addressing the individual as well as the pluralistic nature of services required for families, children, and communities.

A Code of Ethics

I shall maintain as my highest priority, the rights and needs of children while recognizing adult family needs as an important contingency to those of children.

I shall acquire sufficient knowledge to be a public relations advocate for community understanding, support, and respect for and among those carrying out the program of services.

I shall know and accept the defined responsibilities and parameters of my role as a policy/decision maker, responsibilities that are separate from those of program administrators.

I shall endeavor to provide adequate human and financial resources to ensure long-range benefits to families and children rather than to advocate crisis intervention strategies as short-range solutions.

I shall choose a capable administrator who will be accountable for program implementation and contribute professional expertise to those responsible for policy determination.

I shall contribute to the ongoing review, evaluation, and modification of services as needed by the community, families, and children.

To ignore the need to stimulate action within the early childhood profession toward the creation of ethical standards implies a complacency we can ill afford.

Summary

To initiate interest in such a code is only to begin to touch the surface of deep, provocative issues. To ignore the need to stimulate action within the early childhood education, care, and development profession toward the creation of ethical standards, implies a complacency we can ill afford. The professionalization of early childhood education, development, and care continues to occupy serious workers and students in the field. Ethics is clearly an integral part of this larger issue. No comprehension of the needs in the current arena of early education is complete until professionalism, including its component of ethics, has been sufficiently explored.* All who relish the deserved recognition of this profession will reflect on these proposed codes and talk with their peers toward this end.

* * *

The membership of the National Association for the Education of Young Children is the proper arena for the continued pursuit and ultimate adoption of a code of ethics.

References

Association and Society Manager 8, no. 3 (April-May 1976).
Combs, A., et al. *The Professional Education of Teachers.* 2nd ed. Boston: Allyn and Bacon, 1974.
Hechinger, F. "Education." *Saturday Review* 3, no. 3 (November 1975): 27.
Houston, W. R., and Howsam, R. B., eds. *Competency-Based Teacher Education: Progress, Problems, and Prospects.* Chicago: Science Research Associates, 1972.
Lerner, M. "The Shame of the Professions." *Saturday Review* 3, no. 3 (November 1975): 10.
Rivlin, A. M., and Timpane, P. M., eds. *Planned Variation in Education: Should We Give Up or Try Harder?* Washington, D.C.: Brookings Institution, 1975.

---

*Harlene Galen is credited with this linkage.

Selected NAEYC Publications

Code #	Title	Price
214	**Activities for School-Age Child Care,** by Rosalie Blau, Elizabeth H. Brady, Ida Bucher, Betsy Hiteshew, Ann Zavitkovsky, and Docia Zavitkovsky	$3.50
303	**A Beginner's Bibliography**	$ .50
132	**The Block Book,** edited by Elisabeth S. Hirsch	$3.50
213	**Caring: Supporting Children's Growth,** by Rita M. Warren	$2.00
402S	**Cómo Reconocer un Buen Programa de Educación Pre-Escolar**	$ .25
104	**Current Issues in Child Development,** edited by Myrtle Scott and Sadie A. Grimmett	$3.50
313	**Cultural Awareness: A Resource Bibliography,** by Velma Schmidt and Earldene McNeill	$4.75
300	**Early Childhood Education: An Introduction to the Profession,** by James L. Hymes, Jr.	$1.50
215	**A Festival of Films**	$1.75
212	**A Good Beginning for Babies: Guidelines for Group Care,** by Anne Willis and Henry Ricciuti	$4.50
302	**A Guide to Discipline,** by Jeannette Galambos Stone	$1.50
210	**The Idea Box,** by Austin AEYC	$5.75
304	**Ideas That Work with Young Children,** edited by Katherine Read Baker	$3.00
131	**Language in Early Childhood Education,** edited by Courtney B. Cazden	$3.00
101	**Let's Play Outdoors,** by Katherine Read Baker	$1.00
312	**Mother/Child, Father/Child Relationships,** edited by Joseph H. Stevens, Jr., and Marilyn Mathews	$4.75
308	**Mud, Sand, and Water,** by Dorothy M. Hill	$2.00
135	**Parent Involvement in Early Childhood Education,** by Alice S. Honig	$3.00
102	**Piaget, Children, and Number,** by Constance Kamii and Rheta DeVries	$2.00
115	**Planning Environments for Young Children: Physical Space,** by Sybil Kritchevsky and Elizabeth Prescott with Lee Walling	$1.75
306	**Play as a Learning Medium,** edited by Doris Sponseller	$2.75

(continued)

129	**Play: The Child Strives Toward Self-Realization,** edited by Georgianna Engstrom	$2.50
126	**Promoting Cognitive Growth: A Developmental-Interaction Point of View,** by Barbara Biber, Edna Shapiro, David Wickens, in collaboration with Elizabeth Gilkeson	$2.75
307	**Providing the Best for Young Children,** edited by Jan McCarthy and Charles R. May	$3.25
309	**Science with Young Children,** by Bess-Gene Holt	$3.25
128	**The Significance of the Young Child's Motor Development,** edited by Georgianna Engstrom	$2.25
402E	**Some Ways of Distinguishing a Good Early Childhood Program**	$ .25
310	**Talks with Teachers: Reflections on Early Childhood Education,** by Lilian G. Katz	$3.00
305	**Teacher Education,** edited by Bernard Spodek	$2.25
202	**The Young Child: Reviews of Research, Volume I,** edited by Willard W. Hartup and Nancy L. Smothergill	$3.75
207	**The Young Child: Reviews of Research, Volume II,** edited by Willard W. Hartup	$5.75

Order from NAEYC
        1834 Connecticut Avenue, N.W.
        Washington, DC 20009

For information about these and other NAEYC publications, write for a free publications brochure.

**Please enclose full payment for orders under $10.00.
Add 10% handling charge to all orders.**